Smokeheads

DOUG JOHNSTONE

ff

faber and faber

First published in 2011
by Faber and Faber Limited
Bloomsbury House, 74–77 Great Russell Street,
London WC1B 3DA

Typeset by Faber and Faber Ltd
Printed in England by CPI Mackays, Chatham, Kent

The right of Doug Johnstone to be identified as author of this work has been asserted in
accordance with Section 77 of the Copyright, Designs and Patents Act 1988

A CIP record for this book
is available from the British Library

ISBN 978-0-571-26062-1

2 4 6 8 10 9 7 5 3 1

For Aidan and Amber

'Freedom an' whisky gang thegither'
Robert Burns

Blood roared in his ears and his heart thudded as he scrambled across the ice.

Behind him, thousands of heavy shapes filled the night sky and covered the frozen loch, panicked birds creating a mayhem of flapping and crying. From somewhere amongst them a flare sent fingers of violet light searching across the land. He ran on, desperate to escape the nightmare chasing him.

He looked ahead for his friends, but there wasn't enough light to make anything out. He struggled to breathe as panic forced him onwards, his legs aching and head pounding.

There was a low, heavy creak and the ice split up ahead, slivers of black reaching towards his feet. The ice gave way under him and he plunged into freezing water, the breath hammered out of his body.

He grabbed and scratched at broken shards of ice as he went down, the shock of the cold tensing his muscles and sending spasms through him. His head went under and his face burned.

Thrashing his way to the surface with stiff arms, he tried to call out, but his lungs were empty. He sank, gulping water as he went.

His body jerked as he tried to resurface. His chest was ready to burst as he flailed and thrashed through jagged chunks of ice. His head cleared the water and he thought he saw a hand held out towards him.

He tried to reach for it but missed. He felt his body being

dragged back under, the cold sucking the life from him and setting his nerves on fire.

Steeling himself for one last effort, he thrust his body upwards, hoping the hand was still there, hoping someone would save him, hoping there was a way out of this.

He pushed for a final time with every inch of effort he had left, stretching his hands up and out of the water, searching for something to hold on to.

I

'What are we drinking?'

'Take a guess.'

Adam looked at Roddy towering over him, upright and steady despite the wind. They always played this game, Roddy keen to catch out the supposed whisky expert. Adam examined the deep amber liquid in the glass as the wind swirled fiercely around them, the motion of the ferry making him shift his weight. Not the best environment for a tasting, but he stuck his nose in the glass anyway.

It was peppery, splashes of seaweed, a big hit of peat then something sweeter, maybe cinnamon. It would be an Islay, of course, given that they were on the boat to Port Askaig. Adam took a sip and let the spirit roll round his mouth, over and under his tongue, soaking into his taste buds. It was old, too much oak, vanilla and cocoa smoothing out the raw spiciness. It wasn't any of the working distilleries, which left one option.

'Port Ellen?'

Roddy smiled. 'What age?'

'Thirty?'

Roddy sucked his teeth. 'Twenty-seven-year-old. Single cask, limited edition 137 bottles. Set me back 320 quid.'

Typical fucking Roddy, he couldn't give you a dram without letting you know how expensive it was. Typical of him to have Port Ellen as well, the rarest and most over-hyped Islay malt.

That was Roddy all over, style over substance. Adam tried to curb his bile; he would have to stay calm on this trip if he was going to get what he wanted. He looked at his new watch and pressed the button.

'Why do you keep doing that?' said Roddy, glugging whisky and refilling his glass.

Adam hesitated. 'It has a heart-rate monitor on it.'

Roddy laughed theatrically. 'Really?'

'Yeah.'

'And?'

Deep breath. 'Eighty-nine bpm.'

'At rest? Jesus wept, you're a stroke waiting to happen. The last thing you need to be doing is keeping tabs on your bpm, Strachan, you'll worry yourself to death.'

Adam started whispering under his breath – 'Serenity now, serenity now.' It had started as a joke from *Seinfeld* years ago, Roddy comparing Adam to uptight loser George, Adam joining in the laughter so that he was part of the joke rather than the butt of it. Now he was George for real.

'What are you doing now?' said Roddy, peering at him. 'Meditating?'

Adam took another deep breath. 'Just give me a refill, will you?'

He watched his glass fill up. At least Roddy always poured good measures. Adam looked away and tried to imagine his heart pumping slower, his veins and capillaries easing and narrowing.

They were clear of the mainland now, the scabby Porta-kabin of Kennacraig Terminal gone from view but the brown-green stretch of Islay still just a shrouded fist of knuckles in the distance. In this open water they were brutally exposed to the weather: pummelling, icy winds, snowclouds dark as gravestones pressing down on them as their rusting CalMac hulk strained through the sea.

A snapping noise made Adam look up to see a frayed and faded saltire flapping amongst the ship's rotating radar bars and brick-red funnel. He looked back out to sea, his eyes bleary in the bluster. The wind chopped fat lines of white froth out of the inky water and he had a flashback to last night, ill-advisedly sharing a couple of heavy toots with Roddy in the toilets at Amber.

'The venue was another of Roddy's wind-ups, the restaurant attached to the Scotch Whisky Experience, the tourist-trap travesty next to the castle with a whisky-making tour where you travelled through time in a ridiculous dissected cask. At least Roddy hadn't made them do that. Actually, Amber was a pretty decent restaurant if you ignored all the tartan bullshit, which was impossible. How they'd ended up scraping out lines of Roddy's top-drawer nose powder in the bogs, he couldn't recall. Must've been hammering the cask strength. No surprise, given that Roddy was picking up the tab, keen as ever to demonstrate his obscene wealth to anyone in a five-mile radius.

Adam looked at Roddy now and winced. Tall and fit, wavy hair flicking in the wind, he looked like a Hollywood rendition of a heroic frontiersman off to tame the wilderness and win his bride, all square jaw, striking good looks and smouldering stare. Adam caught a glimpse of his own hungover self in a grubby porthole. Chipmunk cheeks and wobbly chin, balding head and a short, stocky body, red-raw eyes behind dated thick-rimmed meeja specs. He was six inches shorter than Roddy, but it felt like more. It was hard to believe they were the same species, never mind the same age.

A bacon roll filled his view.

'Thank God,' he said as Ethan handed it to him, Luke slinking behind and handing one to Roddy.

'You clowns took your time,' said Roddy.

'Truckers, man,' said Luke, as if that explained it. He slouched into a scuffed plastic seat bolted to the deck and chewed lazily. Adam loved the way Luke didn't give a flying fuck whether he made any sense or not. Some pretentious bastards might aim for enigmatic; Luke managed it without realising. His lanky, emaciated body, rough beard, ever-present beanie and stoned placidity added to the accidental guru effect. He was gazing out to sea, then spoke.

'Puffins.'

Adam couldn't see anything except the choppy waters and emerging peat moors of the island.

'And young gannets.'

Adam looked again, thought he maybe saw tiny blades of white dive-bombing the surf, but couldn't be sure.

'Really?' said Ethan, following Luke's gaze.

Ethan was the most normal of them, Mr Average with his supposedly sensible RBS career-ladder computing job, new-build suburban semi in Gilmerton, conventionally pretty but conservative wife, Debs, and full range of Berghaus and North Face to keep the January cold out. He was average height, average weight and his brown hair was even in a carefully combed side parting, for Christ's sake. Adam liked to be con-descending about Ethan's averageness, but who was the mug? Adam rented his tiny Abbeyhill flat, lived alone and still did a job he hated in the arse end of retail at the age of thirty-eight.

But this weekend would change that. The other three thought he was researching a whisky book, the same hypothetical book they'd been taking the piss out of since he mentioned it one messy night two years ago. Truth was, the book had stalled almost before it started. He couldn't decide whether to make it a serious whisky guide, a novel, a memoir or a diatribe about the industry, and had given up months ago around page twelve.

No, he wasn't here for a book but to get Roddy on board with the plan that was going to turn his life around. He'd spoken to the right people, done his research, worked everything out. Now all he needed was the backing, which was where Roddy came in. Adam was going to spring it on him tomorrow at the site he had in mind, hoping the spirit of the weekend would win him over. But he was nervous. He patted his jacket pocket, felt the reassuring thickness of the folded papers in there. He checked his watch. Ninety-two bpm. Jesus, he had to calm down.

He sipped his Port Ellen. Maybe he'd been a bit harsh on it. It was more complex on the palate than he first thought, heather blossom and tar battling it out, and the finish was pleasantly dry and smoky. Nowhere near his top ten, and wildly overrated and overpriced, but a decent dram nonetheless.

'Hey, man,' said Luke, noticing his glass. 'Where's ours?'

'Cool it, hippy,' said Roddy. He produced two more glasses, filled them and handed them to Luke and Ethan. 'There's plenty of this bad boy for everybody.'

Adam gazed at Islay approaching through the squally gloom.

2

Roddy gunned the engine with a shit-eating grin as they sped off the ferry and past the hotel and corner shop that constituted Port Askaig. As they rose steeply away from the harbour past snow-flecked pine and fir, Adam examined the car. It was a huge beast of an Audi, top of the range apparently, an embarrassing display of four-wheeled affluence. Roddy had insisted on bringing it to show off to the locals. At least there was plenty of room for the four of them and their stuff. Thank fuck they hadn't come in his soft-top Porsche or high-end Beemer, both of which were nestling in the garage at his ridiculous Victorian mansion in Merchiston. Roddy made no secret of the fact he didn't have a mortgage on the place, that's what ten years as a fund manager with White Stone Investments got you, enough cash to buy the same postcode as J. K. Rowling, with outdoor hot tub and tennis court thrown in.

'What are the roads like on this rock?' said Roddy. He lurched the car forward to pass a whisky tanker on a bend, then selected the Killers on the futuristic sound system.

Adam gripped the dashboard. 'Unbelievably bad, except for the main road south.'

'Which is the one we need to take, right?'

'We're on it already.'

'This is the good road? Fuck me sideways.'

Adam looked at the speedometer. They were clocking

eighty on a road full of bends and bumps, twisting past small villages and farms.

'Take it easy, will you?' he said.

'We're losing valuable drinking time, Tiger,' said Roddy, swerving to pass an old couple in a Honda.

Adam wondered if there was any ice on the roads as Roddy bombed past another car. Did they have a gritter on the island? They approached a junction too fast and blurred past a sign saying Port Ellen 11 Miles.

They scudded through Bowmore, past the distillery at the bottom of the hill and the strange cylindrical church at the top, then headed inland across flat moor. The road straightened and Roddy floored it, quickly reaching a ton. Adam checked his watch – Ninety-seven bpm. He looked out the window at a familiar chocolate landscape of peat bog and tussocky grass. Now and then they passed trenches dug by peat cutters, thousands of squares of the stuff piled up alongside the trenches like fibrous mud bricks. They passed fields of grazing geese, Adam pointing them out to Luke in the back seat.

'Barnacle,' said Luke. 'Down from Greenland. Fifty thousand of them.' He turned to Roddy. 'Got any decent music, man?'

'Screw you, hippy,' said Roddy, looking in his mirror. 'Aw, fucksticks. Adam, I thought you said there weren't any police in this backwater.'

Adam turned to see the flashing lights of a police car right up their arse.

'I said there weren't many. Well done on finding one within fifteen minutes.'

For a moment it looked like Roddy was going to try out-running them.

'Roddy,' said Ethan from the back, a tremble in his voice. 'Come on, pull over.'

Roddy considered this for a long moment, then took his foot off the pedal. 'OK, Mortgage Boy, have it your way. But I'm waaaaay over the limit if this clown's got a breathalyser, so hold on to your fucking hats.'

They pulled over and sat, the Killers still blasting away.

'Turn that off,' said Luke.

Adam reached for the button and looked at Roddy. 'Just take it easy, OK?'

Roddy stared at him as if he was a stroppy toddler. 'Trust me, kiddo. When have I ever let you down?'

An officer approached the car. Roddy pressed a button and his window whirred open. The occasional snowflake fluttered down outside as the officer filled the window.

'Out, big guy.'

Roddy smiled around the car as if this was all a huge laugh then got out with an exaggerated sigh. Adam leaned over to get a better view. The copper was big and mean-looking, tight muscle under his protective vest. Roddy was gym-fit, but this guy looked like he'd earned his physique in knuckle-fights or the army. He was a few years younger than them and Adam noticed a heavy gold chain round his neck. Was that police regulation?

'Name and address,' said the copper.

'Is there a problem, mate?' said Roddy, smiling like a visiting dignitary amused by quaint local customs.

'I'm not your fucking mate,' said the copper.

'No need for that language, *officer*.'

The copper stopped at that and slowly scoped Roddy up and down. Roddy put on a big gleaming smile at the attention. The copper narrowed his dark, glistening eyes and smiled. Adam looked round in the car and shared a worried glance with Ethan.

'A fucking comedian, aye? Just give me your licence and keep the one-liners for open mic night.'

Roddy handed over his licence and the copper walked to the squad car to radio it in.

'For Christ's sake,' said Adam, 'give it a rest, will you? You're gonna get us all nicked.'

'Relax,' said Roddy as the copper returned. 'It's all in hand.'

'Visiting the island long, Mr Hunter?' The copper handed back the licence.

'Couple of days.'

'Business or pleasure?' the officer asked, throwing a contemptuous look into the car.

'I'm all about the pleasure, officer.'

'Well, watch how you go, the roads are dangerous this time of year, especially the speed you were going.' He dug a pad out of a pocket and began writing. 'Here's your ticket. You were doing at least ninety.'

Roddy looked like he was about to tell the copper that the real speed was three figures when Adam chipped in.

'Sorry, officer,' he said cheerily through the window. 'It won't happen again.'

The copper looked at him as if he was dogshit on his shoe then turned back to Roddy, giving him a hard stare.

'Like I say, watch yourself this weekend. Islay's a pretty wild place. I wouldn't want you getting into any real trouble out here.'

'Thanks for the advice,' said Roddy, bouncing on his heels

then opening the car door.

The copper watched as Roddy started the engine and revved off, spraying gravel behind them.

'For God's sake, Roddy,' said Ethan. 'You're a magnet for trouble.'

'Easy in the back,' said Roddy as he raced through the gears and put the Killers back on.

'I can't believe he didn't breathalyse you,' said Adam. 'Isn't that standard?'

'Fat fucking chance,' said Roddy. 'If he'd tried I would've had him. I could smell a whole fucking distillery on his breath, he's more loaded than we are. I guess that's one of the perks of being the law on an island full of whisky, eh?'

Serenity now. Adam made a conscious effort not to look at his watch as they headed past a tiny dreich airstrip then more expanses of bleak bracken.

Luke hunched forward between Adam and Roddy.

'Can we *please* listen to some decent music, man,' he said.

3

They walked round the crescent of Port Ellen's main street, a slate sea and gritty beach to their left, a row of twee, white-washed fishermen's cottages on the right. Snowclouds were breaking up into a dappled sky as a sharp westerly brought salty freshness to their noses.

As the only previous visitor, Adam was tour guide. They'd already dumped their bags in the B&B at the other end of Frederick Crescent and were heading to the closer of the town's two pubs for a liquid lunch. After that the plan was to head out the coast road for some distillery visits. Laphroaig, Lagavulin and Ardbeg were all within four miles. Three of the best whiskies in the world, all made on the same stretch of remote, craggy coastline. Adam could taste the peat and seaweed already, or maybe that was the finish of Roddy's single-cask Port Ellen still on his tongue.

The Ardview Inn was indistinguishable from neighbouring B&Bs and homes, sea-blasted white walls and black window frames, stunted palm tree planted in a half barrel across the road. As they approached, a slim figure came outside and lit up. She was young and tall with a long mess of scraggy black hair, and she shivered against the wind in skinny T-shirt and combats.

'Aye, aye,' said Roddy. 'High Street honey at twelve o'clock.'

The rest of them had already noticed, of course, but only Roddy would comment. As they reached the door she lifted a shoulder to let them past, Roddy going first, passing close and eyeballing.

'Hi, there,' he said, lingering at the door.

She raised a weary eyebrow and put on a smile that said she had his number.

Roddy checked her out a moment longer then fired in, the rest in his wake.

Inside, four locals turned and stared. An old couple with collapsed faces and blood-burst noses turned back to their cloudy half-and-a-halfs, two younger guys in Meatloaf and Maiden sweatshirts getting back to swapping bullshit over shiny Kawasakis in a magazine. Adam looked at his watch and resisted the urge to press the button.

'Grab a seat, amigos,' said Roddy, 'I'll get them in.'

They sat at a scuffed wooden bench with shiny grey leatherette padding.

'So what's the plan, like?' said Luke.

Adam grinned and rubbed his hands together.

'Couple of distillery visits this afternoon,' he said. 'Laphroaig, Ardbeg and Lagavulin are all just along the coast, I thought we'd take in a couple of them.'

Ethan nodded keenly. 'Did you see that Ardbeg's Uigeadail got World Whisky of the Year in Jim Murray's new *Whisky Bible*?'

Adam snorted. 'That old hack is obsessed with Ardbeg. There are eight bloody pages of Ardbeg in there. Don't get me wrong, Uigeadail is a fine malt but the basic ten-year-old is better, so's that Corryvreckan they've been punting.'

'Have you tasted Lord of the Isles?' said Ethan.

Adam nodded. 'Way more fruity than the others, cherries

and tangerines. Stupidly overpriced, though, it's £200 in the distillery shop.'

'That Ardbeg at the Society was the business, man,' Luke drawled.

It always surprised Adam what a good memory Luke had, considering how much he toked. All four of them were members of the Scotch Malt Whisky Society back in Edinburgh where they had nights out every couple of months, usually at the ancient Vaults bondhouse in Leith or occasionally in the corporate-whore cash-in joint on Queen Street. A few months back they'd tried a young first-fill sherry-butt Ardbeg, only nine years old but complex and challenging.

Their expeditions to the Society were just about the only time they saw each other these days, twenty years on from when they'd first met as fellow maths students at Edinburgh Uni, four outsiders who didn't fit the geeky cliques and nerdy stereotypes. Over those years their lives had drifted apart, but their love of whisky had somehow kept them tethered together, that and a shared reluctance to give up entirely on the promise of their teenage years.

Adam looked around the bar. The low ceiling and small windows made it feel like they were in a ship's hold, with wood panelling, battered chairs, seafaring memorabilia and cheap tiles all straight out of the seventies. There was an acrid stench coming from the bogs. He'd been in here a few times on previous visits to the island, only for a nightcap, as he didn't like nursing a pint on his own, especially when the locals were all shitfaced. Why expose yourself to that when you've got a bottle of quality malt back at the B&B?

He'd been six times in the last ten years, always on his

own, a busman's holiday away from the shop. He'd worked at Edinburgh Whiskies all that time and had talked about leaving for most of it. The shop sat amongst all the tartan tat sellers at the top of the Royal Mile, and as a result made most of its money selling Bell's miniatures, whisky fudge and malt-scented soap to ignorant tourists. They actually stocked some of the best malts in the world, but trying to get vacant-headed visitors interested was like pulling teeth. He got plenty of perks – free tastings, staff discount and occasional jollies to industry events – but that didn't compensate for the daily grind of explaining the basics to arseholes, and punting shortbread and branded golf balls. Adam grimaced as he pictured his daily walk to work up the length of the Royal Mile, trudging past the endless string of garish, embarrassing tourist traps, elbowing through gangs of foreigners taking pictures of crumbling buildings, a dark cloud over his head the whole way.

All the time he'd worked there he'd never made it near management, always been passed over. He knew he wasn't a team player; he couldn't give a fuck about promotional campaigns or innovative stock control methods or whatever, so he wasn't surprised. These days his boss was an amiable Canadian with a beer belly and a mullet, and he worked alongside a student with model looks who spoke Japanese, German and Swedish, and a keen little shit doing night classes in business management.

He looked over at the bar. Roddy was chatting away to the girl from outside, who turned out to be the barmaid. Her body language was aloof but she was smiling as he leaned over to her, then she laughed and played with her hair as he offered his money.

'He's well coked, man,' said Luke, following Adam's gaze. 'Still buzzing from last night?'

All of them had been invited to Amber, Roddy's idea of a pre-weekend whisky warm-up, but Ethan and Luke had perhaps wisely declined. Adam had a vague memory of stumbling out of the place into a taxi, leaving Roddy chatting to a waitress as the place closed up.

'Could be.'

'He needs to calm down,' said Ethan.

'Fat chance,' said Adam.

Roddy quit flirting and brought the drinks over. Adam noticed the barmaid checking out Roddy's arse as he walked towards them. Jesus, how did he do it?

'Man, that is one dirty little minx,' said Roddy.

'Don't be a twat,' said Adam. 'You only spoke for two minutes.'

'Long enough.'

'Did you even get her name?'

'I did as it happens. Ash.'

'And how did it go with the waitress last night? Can you remember her name?'

Roddy gave him a pitying look. 'Her name was Julie. I should remember, I was howling it all night long.'

'You were up all night?' said Ethan.

Roddy nodded. 'In both senses of the word, Mortgage Boy. A few lines and a couple of little blues.'

Adam knew he shouldn't ask, but couldn't help himself. 'Little blues?'

'Viagra, you fuckwit, get with the twenty-first century.'

'You take Viagra?'

'Got to keep up with the ching. Hard as a fucking brick for six hours. Still got a semi now.'

Roddy didn't have an off button, no sense of embarrassment could penetrate his shield of self-delusion. On the other hand, he was the millionaire at the table, so maybe the delusion was all Adam's.

He couldn't resist. 'And how's Imogen? Wedding plans going fine?'

Roddy didn't flinch. 'Midge is great, thanks. And yes, plans for the nuptials are proceeding apace. Invites will be in the post in a few weeks. I know what you're getting at, Mr High Ground, but it's human nature, I'm just sowing my last few wild oats before taking the final plunge.'

'So all this will stop when you've got a ring on your finger?'

Roddy grinned. 'Of course.'

Only Roddy would have the bollocks to screw around behind the back of a gorgeous model fiancée, but then only Roddy could've got a gorgeous model fiancée in the first place.

Roddy pointed at the table. He'd bought four double nips. 'Come on, then, gaylords,' he said.

They went through the routine of eyeing and swirling, nosing then sipping. Adam looked at the bar. It was only a crappy wee local but they had dozens of malts on the gantry. Whisky was soaked into every facet of life on Islay, eight distilleries amid a population of only three thousand producing millions of gallons of the stuff every year, generating billions of pounds which all left the island to multinational owners in Italy, Japan and America.

They guessed in turn. Ethan nailed his maker, Caol Ila, but

not the age, while Luke was way off with his Bruichladdich seven-year-old Waves, guessing at Bowmore. Luke didn't really have the palate for tasting but didn't seem to give a shit; he liked the whole vibe. Ethan was better but a bit trainspottery, while Roddy didn't care as long as he got to flash his cash and buy them. Adam took another sip. It was smoky, all right, and salty, but something wasn't quite right. There was a shitload of spice and pepper in there, chocolate too. Then it clicked.

'Talisker,' he said as Roddy beamed. Skye whisky, not Islay.

'Thought I'd get you by going off the island. What age?'

Adam sipped again. Not the basic ten, but not a pensioner either. 'Eighteen?'

'Spot on,' said Roddy and raised his glass. 'Here's to a great fucking weekend.'

They all clinked.

'And to unleashing a couple of little blues on that number over there,' he said, nodding at the barmaid.

4

'Man, what a stink,' said Luke as they poured out of the Audi into the Laphroaig car park.

Adam smiled. It was the first thing that struck him every time he visited, the pungent aroma, an overpowering blend of smoked fish, seaweed, tar, peat and iodine, a belt at the back of his sinuses that felt like home.

'That's the antiseptic smell of success,' he said. 'The best whisky in the world. Thought we might as well start at the top.'

They sauntered down the slope towards the sprawl of sturdy whitewashed buildings, pagoda roofs puffing hazily into a silent sky.

'Hey, what's your obsession with Laphroaig?' said Luke as they walked behind the other two. 'You're always banging on about it.'

'You know what it tastes like,' said Adam. 'It's just a huge dram. The biggest balls in the world. It's not afraid to smack you in the face, you know? It's not a fruity Speyside or a heathery Highland, it's sea and sand and sky and peat and everything that's great about Scotland. Part-time drammers hate it, that's good enough for me.'

'Dude, you are such a whisky snob.'

'I just appreciate when things are done right.'

Luke chuckled. 'You're ridiculous, man, the things you get worked up about. It's just booze.'

Adam stopped, turned and pressed a finger into Luke's chest, only half joking. 'It is not just fucking booze. You don't believe that any more than I do, or you wouldn't be on this trip.'

'I'm just here for the ride, mate, take it easy.'

They walked on, a beautiful rocky cove emerging behind the buildings, tufted crags flanking a sheltered natural harbour of icy blackness.

'Listen, man,' said Luke. 'When are we gonna find ourselves some peatreek?'

Adam raised his eyebrows.

'Hey, I can google,' said Luke. 'This island has a fine reputation for illegal hooch over the years. I want to taste some moonshine, get a bit of that bootleg action.'

Adam shook his head. 'It's just a myth, I don't think there are illicit stills here any more.'

'Come on, the history of this place? I bet there are hundreds of farmhouses and sheds on the island pumping out new spirit as we speak. You've been here before, you must've heard rumours.'

'Occasionally, but that's all they are.'

Luke smiled to himself as they reached the waterfront. 'You just need to get a bit more friendly with the natives, man. I'm telling you, I'm gonna taste peatreek before this weekend is over.'

They caught up with Roddy and Ethan and stared out to sea. Two large black birds flapped low across the bay and out towards open water.

'Cormorants,' said Luke.

Adam pointed to a low dark hummock in the far distance. 'See that? Northern Ireland.'

'Wow, are we that close?' said Ethan.

'About thirty miles.'

Ethan turned round to face the distillery. 'Check it out.'

They all turned to see LAPHROAIG painted in thick black lettering twelve feet high on a huge white wall. Ethan pulled out his phone and took a quick snapshot as they gazed at the humungous sign.

Adam thought about all the history soaked into the buildings here. Two hundred years since the place was established by a couple of farming brothers on the make, and hundreds more years of under-the-radar distilling before that. Generations of families had dedicated their lives to making whisky here, lived and died with the smell of the place permeating their bones, the peaty taste of it on their lips from cradle to grave.

He reached into his pocket and rubbed the folded sheets of paper in there between his fingers, thinking about what might happen tomorrow when he put the whole idea to Roddy. His chest rose and fell with a sharp breath.

'OK, pooves,' said Roddy, breaking the silence. 'Let's get inside and drink some of this shit, shall we?'

5

The visitor centre was empty, an untended bar and reception area swathed in the racing green and white of the distillery's logo. Shelves of spotlit bottles, clothing, glassware and other tourist guff lined the walls.

'Hey, no fuck's home,' said Roddy, slinking behind the bar. 'Reckon we can help ourselves?'

He lifted a bottle of thirty-year-old from the gantry and pretended to neck it. As he was doing a comedy glugging motion the door behind him swung open and a woman walked through. She was early thirties, short and curvy with long fair hair cut in a no-nonsense fringe and tied back. She wore a branded green T-shirt and short black skirt, show-ing off full breasts and shapely legs. She had green eyes that matched the Laphroaig bottles and a kind smile which faded when she spotted Roddy dicking around. She tilted her head at a reproachful angle and put out a hand.

'If you don't mind?'

Roddy handed over the bottle and sauntered out from behind the bar. 'Just mucking about.'

'So I see.' She had a soft accent, a lilting rhythm to every word. She returned the bottle to the gantry, turned and spotted Adam.

'Oh, hi there,' she said, her smile switching back on. 'Haven't seen you for a while. Adam, right?'

'Right,' said Adam, feeling his cheeks flush a little. 'Yeah, I don't think you were working last time I was here.'

'When was that?' she said, leaning on the bar.

'April, I think.'

Her eyes darkened a moment. 'Yeah, took some time off around then. Needed a break.' She refocused on the room. 'You here for the weekend?'

Adam nodded.

'And you've brought company this time, I see.'

'Sorry about this idiot, we can't take him anywhere.'

She waved it away. There was a moment's awkward pause.

'So, are you wanting to go on the tour? I mean, I know *you* know all about the place, but for the rest of them?'

'Exactly,' said Adam. 'We're doing a few distilleries while we're here, I thought we'd start with the best.'

She raised her eyebrows. 'Bet you say that to all the tour guides.'

Adam flushed again.

'Next tour starts in ten minutes,' she said, looking at her watch. 'You can wait in the lounge, since you're a Friend.'

'Thanks.'

Adam led the others into a separate room with plush leather sofas and casks for tables. As they walked, Roddy nudged him in the ribs.

'Well?'

'What?'

'Don't be fucking coy,' said Roddy. 'All this time, you've had a woman stashed on Islay.'

'Molly?'

'Is that her name?'

30

'I think so.'

Roddy laughed. 'Fuck off, you know so. She remembers you, anyway.'

'So?'

'So? How many times have you met?'

'I dunno, two or three. Maybe four.'

'And when was the last time?'

'Piss off with the interrogation, Roddy.'

'When?'

'The whisky festival they have here on the island, the year before last. Eighteen months ago, I suppose.'

'A year and a half and she remembers your name? You are *so* in there.'

Adam sighed. 'She's a distillery tour guide, Roddy, she's paid to be nice to visitors.'

'I bet she doesn't remember everyone's name, though, does she? And she called you a friend.'

Adam smiled. 'That's Friend with a capital "F". It's a gimmick where you sign up online and get a square foot of peat bog or something. I only joined to get priority on new expressions.'

Roddy started singing. 'Adam and Molly up a tree, F-U-C-K-I-N-G . . .'

'Shut the hell up,' said Adam, punching his arm and looking round. 'She'll hear you.'

'You like her,' said Roddy in a childish voice.

Adam rolled his eyes. 'This isn't primary school, Roddy. Besides, she's married.'

'How do you know?'

'She mentioned her husband last time I met her.'

'That means fuck all,' said Roddy. 'She's probably just playing hard to get or warding off psychos. Midge is always telling guys she's married to get them to back off. Anyway, eighteen months is a long time, a lot can happen in a year and a half.'

They were joined in the lounge by three bald, geeky guys dressed like Arctic explorers.

'Swedes,' whispered Luke as Roddy continued to goad Adam.

'How can you tell?' said Ethan, but Luke just shrugged.

Adam looked over at Molly behind the counter. He'd first met her a few years back when she'd given him the tour here, Adam lurking amongst Japanese and German visitors. She was friendly and liberal with the measures at the end of the tour, and he'd lingered and chatted after the others had gone. She knew her stuff, knew all about the history of whisky on the island and the chemistry of distillation, but more importantly she had a wide smile, shining eyes and a bottle of twenty-five-year-old in her hand.

Ever since then he'd looked out for her, his heart sagging a little if she wasn't working. He hadn't seen her on a couple of visits and had almost forgotten about her by the time he visited the whisky festival the year before last. When he spotted her at the Laphroaig stall she'd been as friendly and chatty as ever, but his heart sank again when she mentioned her husband.

Not that he thought for a minute he'd ever have a chance with her – she was younger than him, better looking and full of life and smiles. Why would she be interested in a cynical dramhead like him? And besides, she lived here on the island, several hours by road and ferry from Edinburgh. Anyway, he would never have the bottle to make a move on her, so it was entirely hypothetical. Then again, there was the big plan he had in his pocket. If Roddy went for it, Adam would be spending a whole lot more time on Islay, time he could use to get to know Molly better. He shook his head as he felt his heart race; he was getting way ahead of himself as usual.

Molly checked her watch and made her way to the lounge. She had a comfortable, sexy walk, a lack of self-consciousness that Adam envied. She grinned warmly at him then addressed the room.

'This way for the tour, gentlemen,' she said, holding open a large door.

Roddy slid up to Adam. 'Spot that?'

'What?'

Roddy made a goon face and pointed at a finger on his left hand. 'No ring, Loverboy. She's not wearing a fucking ring.'

6

Adam drifted through the tour in a haze. He knew the workings of the distillery inside out, and found himself staring at Molly's left hand, gazing at her beautiful eyes and sneaking glances at the contours of her body.

Molly had the tour spiel polished and slick as sea glass. She led them round the malthouse where tonnes of green barley were steeped in water then laid out to germinate on the floor. They saw the kilns where the malted barley was smoked over a huge peat fire, each of them chucking a lump of the stuff in. The cloggy smell and fierce heat from the furnace were remarkable. At the mill they tasted the malt, little seeds that burst with smoky flavour in their mouths. Adam watched as Molly chewed along with the rest of them. They saw the grist mixed with water and turned to wort in the mash tun then combined with yeast in the washbacks. They all had a glug of the liquid, a warm, yeasty eight per cent beer that had the Swedes making surprised faces. Ethan got his phone out and snapped the rest of them necking the stuff.

Then the wash was fired into the stills, seven huge bulbous copper constructions with swan necks, surrounded by gangways and pipes in the large stillhouse. The double distillation made low wines in the wash still which were pumped into the spirit still then boiled off into the spirit safe, a Victorian brass box with levers where the stillman had to siphon off the drinkable middle cut between the foreshots and the feints.

Adam smiled as Molly rolled the terminology around her tongue. He loved the unique language of the whisky-maker, the depths of ancient knowledge about the craft that those words contained. Molly mentioned in passing that only nine people were employed in the actual whisky-making at Laphroaig, producing two million litres of pure spirit a year, a fact Adam found astonishing every time he heard it. How could such a hugely lucrative operation rely on just a few experienced souls?

From the stillhouse they visited the filling store to see new spirit pumped into casks, air-dried American oak, first-fill Maker's Mark bourbon casks which lent the whisky its vanilla and caramel nuances. They each got a sip of new spirit, sixty-eight per cent by volume making their eyes water. It was raw and rough but discernibly Laphroaig already, even before maturation.

At the warehouse on the edge of the seaweed-strewn bay Molly fielded questions from the Swedes about phenolic ppm in the barley, tannins and lignins from the barrels, the percentage of taste that came from the terroir compared to wine. The Swedes knew their stuff but Molly wasn't flustered. Even though they all knew, she told them about the angel's share, the two per cent lost per year from the barrels due to evaporation, adding up to a shitload of whisky vanishing into the atmosphere and contributing to the pungent air around them.

Adam felt light-headed for a moment. The burn of the new spirit was still in his nostrils as he watched Roddy joke with Molly about rolling a barrel out of the warehouse and into his car. He ran a hand over a nearby cask. The date on it was

36

1995, already past the ten-year bottling stage and heading for something richer and more complex. He thought about the to and fro inside, the spirit and the oak from different sides of the world blending and lending flavours to each other, mingling to create something utterly unique. That was partly why he loved whisky: for all the science involved there were completely un-predictable factors, influences that made two adjacent casks of the same spirit turn into whiskies with different characters. Even the location by the sea made a difference – if the whisky inside could evaporate, surely some of this briny air could seep into the casks? Much was made of the subtleties of winemaking, but to his mind whisky distilling was infinitely more complex, with a wider variety of influencing factors and a far greater range of tastes in the end product.

His finger snagged on the rough wood of the cask. He lifted it and saw a dark skelf lodged under the skin. He tried to pick it out but couldn't get any purchase.

'Looks like Roddy's moving in on your turf.' It was Ethan next to him. Adam followed his gaze to see Roddy still flirting with Molly. He felt a twinge in his finger, a soft throb beneath the surface.

'She's not my turf,' he said. 'She's not anyone's turf, she's married.'

He thought about the lack of a ring on her finger and found himself walking towards her. She looked up and he thought he saw something in her eyes, something meaningful.

'I was just telling your friend here it's time for a tasting,' she said.

'Perfect,' said Adam.

Molly corralled them out of the warehouse and across the

courtyard back to the visitor centre. She brought out a tray of nosing glasses and lifted bottles of ten-year-old and quarter cask down from the shelf. She poured out healthy measures and they all went through the rigmarole, checking the colour and legs, taking a noseful then a sip. The Swedes monopolised her with more questions about tasting notes, expressions and rare bottlings.

Roddy sidled up to Adam as he drank. 'Well?'

'Well what?'

'You gonna make a move, Loverboy?'

Adam shook his head. 'You're like a dog with a bone, Roddy.'

'A boner, more like.' Roddy looked down at his own crotch, Adam following his gaze.

'Made you look,' Roddy laughed. 'Fucking hellfire, you think I'd be walking about a distillery with a hard-on?'

'Nothing would surprise me.'

'You crack me up, Tiger.' Roddy slapped his back.

'What do you think?' said Ethan coming over.

'About what?' said Adam.

Ethan raised his glass. 'The quarter cask. It's pretty special, isn't it?'

'Too sweet for me,' said Adam. 'Laphroaig doesn't need bloody citrus overtones.'

Roddy snorted and shook his head. 'Never mind all that shit, what about the cute girl?'

'What about her?'

'Just go talk to her.'

'What about?'

'What do you fucking think? Whisky, you dolt.'

'She's busy with the Swedes.'

'Oh, for fuck's sake.' Roddy raised his head. 'Hey, Molly.'

She looked thankful for the interruption, made her excuses and headed over. 'Yes?'

Adam pressed the button on his watch. Ninety-nine bpm. Shit.

'We're looking to party tonight,' said Roddy. 'Any idea where four guys might find a bit of action on this island?'

Molly smiled. 'It's not exactly party central. Where are you staying?'

'B&B in Port Ellen.'

'The Ardview is your best bet on a Friday night. You know it?'

'Sure, we've been in already. What are you up to this evening? Fancy joining us for a wee snifter?'

Molly looked from Roddy to Adam, then back again. Adam felt the skelf in his finger ache. 'Actually I've already got plans to meet my sister in there tonight. Maybe I'll see you at the bar.'

'It's a date,' said Roddy. 'Looking forward to it.'

Molly began tidying as they finished their drams, the Swedes cornering her for more information.

'There, that wasn't so difficult, was it?' said Roddy.

'It's not a date.'

'We're meeting her and her no doubt equally cute sister in the pub, it doesn't matter what you fucking call it. It's a gold-plated snatch opportunity is what it is.'

Adam looked at Molly, who smiled at him. He looked at her hand on the Laphroaig bottle, definitely no ring. He looked at his own finger and noticed the skelf had worked its way a little deeper under the skin. He was never going to get it out now.

7

Adam lifted an embossed leather dog collar from a shelf. The Ardbeg gift shop took branded tat to a whole new level. Cufflinks, memory sticks, rucksacks and little tins of peat cones, there was nothing they couldn't stamp their wee Celtic logo on. He threw the collar down and walked back to the table where Luke was slouched, drumming his fingers on a menu.

The other two had gone on the tour, but Adam and Luke had stopped in the Old Kiln Cafe to grab something to eat. Ethan had been keen to see round the distillery, Roddy joining him when he saw the tall, perky redhead taking the tour. Adam had been round the place before, of course, and besides, he wanted a bit of time to think about Molly.

Roddy had been a total dick back at Laphroaig, but you couldn't argue with his results. They were on for joining Molly and her sister in the pub tonight, and the absence of a wedding ring made Adam reassess his chances from zero to almost zero.

His lack of success with women was legendary amongst the gang, Roddy never missing an opportunity to rub it in. He'd never had a relationship lasting more than a few months, which for someone with one eye on forty was pretty worrying. He was plenty interested, but always overcome by a crippling lack of confidence, his psyche riddled with self-doubt. Not the most appealing trait in a boyfriend, he had to admit. In contrast, Roddy was all cock and balls, ploughing his way through the female population of Scotland, it seemed. Ethan had been like Adam at uni, never getting anywhere, but that changed when Debs took him on and quickly moulded him into typical husband material. As for Luke, he never mentioned women, and there was something in that silence which meant the rest of them never asked. Adam couldn't remember him with a girlfriend since uni, but then he spent all his time these days at his remote farmhouse-cum-studio, doing soundtrack work for television and film, or creating that strange chilled-out electronica of his.

He was the enigma of the group, the one who never really talked about his life. Once or twice Adam had spotted the name Luke Young in the end credits of television shows, original score or sound editor, and wondered how he'd made the leap into that from his maths degree. They'd all wound up doing something pretty removed from their official qualification, but Luke's career as musician and composer was the furthest out there.

Adam had only ever been to his house a few times, a secluded sprawl of old buildings along a farm track outside Pencaitland. Luke had bought the place, gutted it and transformed it into a studio, using the insurance money he received when his mum and dad died. His parents had been poor and his childhood was much more deprived than the other three, brought up in a poky flat in Tranent as opposed to their smarter houses in Gullane, Haddington and North Berwick – all the more affluent en-claves of East Lothian. But when Mr and Mrs Young were hit by a drunk driver and killed on the way back from the so-cial club one night not long after Luke's graduation, it emerged they'd had a healthy life-insurance policy stashed away, enough to pay off their mortgage and leave Luke with a big lump sum.

After the painful process of clearing out and selling his folks' house, he went travelling on his own for a year, trekking round the snowy expanses of the Arctic countries, across Greenland and the northern reaches of Canada, long visits to Iceland and the Faroes, even spending some time on the Svalbard archipelago. Not that Adam and the rest got much out of him about his travels except for the odd postcard. He returned with a noticeable sense of peace over what had happened to his family and a metal plate in the back of his skull thanks to a snowmobile accident in a Swedish blizzard. That's when the beanie hats started, to cover the extensive scarring to his crown, along with a steady grass habit to combat the occasional migraines. He was quieter and more reserved than he'd been before, but also more comfortable with his new place in the world.

He'd thrown himself into the studio project, transforming it from derelict outhouses to high-tech operation in eighteen months, and had split the time since then between making his own music and building up a reputation for atmospheric soundscapes perfect for edgy dramas and documentaries.

Adam envied the way Luke never got worked up about anything, the way he seemed so assured, confident and happy about everything in his life. He looked at him now, content to sit there tapping along to a song in his head. He noticed the lazy left eye, and underneath the scruffy beard he could make out the pale curve of scar tissue on his chin, the result of a drunken accident with a pint glass years ago that none of them could remember properly.

Luke was his own boss and earned a living doing something he loved. That was what Adam wanted. Luke had partly

43

been the inspiration for Adam's big idea, the real reason they were on Islay this weekend. He'd planned to spring it on the rest of them tomorrow, but he was suddenly itching to talk about it now.

'Luke, you know when you built your studio?'

Luke nodded, though maybe he was just nodding to the sounds in his head.

'Was it a nightmare? I mean logistically?'

Luke played with a leather bracelet on his wrist.

'Not easy, man. Planning and managing, that's not my bag. Best thing I ever did, though. Changed my life.'

Adam nodded and smiled. 'How about being your own boss? Doesn't that take a lot of organisation?'

Luke gazed into the distance for a while. 'Worth it, if you love what you do.'

Adam wanted Luke to ask why he was asking, to draw his plans out of him, but Luke was silent. Maybe it could wait till tomorrow. Tonight he had Molly to think about. He felt a trill in his chest at the thought of seeing her later and resisted the urge to check his heart rate.

'What do you think of Molly?' he said.

Luke was back to fiddling with the thing on his wrist. 'Seems cool.'

'Do you think I should go for it?'

'Why not?'

'She's pretty cute, eh?'

'Yeah.'

Adam examined Luke for a moment. 'You know, you don't talk about your love life at all.'

Luke smiled and shrugged.

'You got a lady tucked away somewhere we don't know about?'

'Not as such.'

'What does that mean?'

Luke just shrugged again and picked up a menu. 'Can we eat? I'm starving.'

Adam smiled then shook his head.

'Fucking lezzer.' It was Roddy and Ethan approaching the table and laughing.

Ethan nodded towards the redhead tour guide, tidying away tasting glasses across the hall. 'Roddy struck out and he's taking it badly.'

'I'm telling you, I know a carpetmuncher when I see one.'

Ethan shook his head. 'Maybe she just didn't fancy you.'

Roddy looked at him as if he'd grown a second head. 'Don't ever fucking say that to me again.'

Adam and Luke joined in the laughter as Ethan sat down, making an 'L' for 'loser' with his thumb and index finger on his forehead.

'Fuck the lot of you,' said Roddy, laughing as well now. 'Shower of cunts.'

He looked around the cafe. 'What do you have to do to get a fucking drink around here?'

8

The Ardview was busy, a bustle of post-work Friday drinkers creating a growl of noise and laughter. Everyone seemed to know everyone. Each time the door opened, new arrivals were greeted with friendly antagonism and abuse, like *Cheers* with hard-earned, liver-damaged cynicism instead of one-liners.

Adam stood listening to Roddy chat up the barmaid from earlier, who'd finished her shift. She was slumped on a barstool glugging double JD and smiling sarcastically. No sign of Molly. Adam turned at the sound of the door as two thick-armed blokes in mechanics' overalls came in.

They'd left Ethan and Luke at the B&B, Ethan on his mobile to Debs, Luke doing something on a laptop, both promising to head over soon.

Adam looked at Ash. She was cute in a gawky kind of way, but looked exhausted, dark bags under her eyes. The exposed skin on her back, neck and arms was tattooed with flowing interlaced Celtic designs. Adam stared at them, trying to make sense of the swirling patterns.

Ash downed her drink and Roddy offered to get another. How could anyone on Islay drink Jack fucking Daniel's when they had the best whisky in the world on their doorstep? JD wasn't even a proper bourbon, made in the wrong American state using the wrong techniques and tasting like a mouthful of iron filings. You might as well drink Whyte and fucking Mackay.

Roddy waved a fifty-pound note at the big bear of a barman, who ignored him. Ash turned to Adam.

'You two known each other long?' She sounded wasted already.

'Too long,' said Adam. 'Twenty years.'

'Jesus.' She laughed, throwing her head back. She had a sharp laugh but her eyes were cloudy. 'And you've put up with him all that time?'

Adam laughed. 'To be fair, most of that time we've been pretty drunk.'

Ash smiled. 'I'll drink to that.' She raised her glass then frowned when she realised it was empty.

Roddy appeared with drinks.

'My hero,' Ash cooed, taking the JD and gulping.

'Been talking about me?' said Roddy.

'I was asking your friend how you got to be such a cocky bastard,' said Ash.

'Years of practice,' Roddy said, then tapped his pocket. 'And some assistance from good old Uncle Charlie.'

Ash raised an eyebrow.

'Interested in meeting him?'

Was he really offering coke to a barmaid he'd known for five minutes?

Ash smiled. 'I think we'll get along famously. Follow me.'

She walked to the toilets with a well-practised slinky move of her hips. Roddy glanced at Adam and pointed at his pocket.

'Three's a crowd,' said Adam.

Roddy set off behind Ash, bounding like a puppy.

Adam hated being left alone in the pub, but he wanted to keep his head straight for Molly, didn't want any of that coke bullshit clouding his thinking. Where the hell were Ethan and Luke? He checked his watch, just gone half seven. He pressed the button – 90 bpm. Actually, that wasn't bad.

He leant on the bar and examined the gantry. They really did have an impressive collection of malts, dozens of familiar and rare bottles neatly lined up. Something caught his eye towards the far end, a squat, stunted bottle with 'X4+1' in large lettering on a plain black label. He'd never seen it before; it didn't seem to have a distillery logo.

'Deliverance.'

Adam turned. It was the old guy with the blood-burst nose who'd been in with his wife at lunchtime. He nodded towards the bottle Adam had been looking at.

'What?'

'Bruichladdich Deliverance, from the Feis Ile.'

Adam hadn't been at the most recent whisky festival, that's why he didn't recognise it. Must be a special bottling.

'What's the X4+1 all about?'

'Quadruple distilled, one year old.'

'What? That's insane.'

He'd never heard anything like it. What the fuck were Bruichladdich doing selling one-year-old spirit? They couldn't even call it whisky till it had lived in a barrel for three years. And quadruple distilled? He knew they were doing some experimental shit up there, but that was ridiculous.

The old man nodded slowly.

'I'm going to have to try some of that,' said Adam.

The man sucked his teeth. 'It's not cheap. Eight bar a nip.'

'Fuck it.' Adam waved the barman over. 'Give me a nip of that Deliverance stuff.'

He looked apologetically at the old man. 'I would get you one, but . . .'

The old man raised his hand, waved a large dram at him. 'I'm fine with this.'

The barman clunked the shot on the table and Adam paid. He nosed it – toffee and candyfloss, very woody. It was powerful stuff. He took a sip and got an explosion of fruit, apricot and peach, liquorice folding into a fizzy sensation like lemonade. The finish was like cheap sweets full of E numbers, somehow spicy too.

'Wow, that's one weird dram.'

'Aye,' said the old man.

Adam examined the glass. 'You think quadruple distilling will catch on?'

The old man sighed. 'Stranger things have happened.'

Adam looked at him. 'What do you think of what they're doing up there?'

The old man shrugged. 'Fair play to 'em, they're bringing the whole thing into the new millennium, aren't they?'

'I thought you'd be against them pissing about with the island's tradition.'

The old man laughed. 'Tradition? Half these places were mothballed for years, and before that almost every Islay whisky got used for cheap blends anyway.'

'Yeah, but you've been making whisky here for centuries.'

'Aye, often undrinkable shite.' The man broke off with a racking cough, like his lungs were mutinying.

'So you're in favour of new operations starting up, then?'

The old man nodded. 'If they use local expertise and stay as part of the community, where's the harm? The big guys pump all their money off the island at the moment. What we need are local businesses adding to the economy here on the island. Every new distillery brings the tourists in, no bad thing for the Ileach.'

Adam took another sip of Deliverance. It was a complete shock to his palate.

The old man coughed again, snorting and gagging a little.

'Time for a fag,' he mumbled. He picked up a rolly tin and headed towards the door.

Adam turned back to the bar and examined his glass for a moment, letting the white noise of the pub wash over him.

'All alone?'

He turned to see Molly in a long green parka. She pulled the hood down and ran a hand through her hair, which fell in long curves to her shoulders.

'Hi,' said Adam, suddenly self-conscious. 'Yeah, Roddy's just gone to the loo, the other two are still at the B&B.'

Molly smiled. 'And you wanted to get a head start, eh?'

'Something like that.' Adam looked round. 'Where's your sister?'

Molly followed his gaze. 'Meeting her here. She'll be lurking in the shadows. She's never far from a drink.'

Adam fought the urge to look at his heart rate. 'What can I get you?'

'Pint of Nerabus, thanks.'

'What?'

Molly pointed to an Islay Ales tap at the bar. 'Nerabus. A winter warmer.'

He'd seen the ale taps earlier but hadn't got one, scared Roddy would take the piss out of him for being an old fogey. He downed what was left of his Deliverance, sending a shudder slithering through his neck and shoulders, and ordered two Nerabus. When he turned back Molly had her coat off. She was wearing a long-sleeved top with a Dangermouse T-shirt over it.

'I used to love Dangermouse,' said Adam, staring at her breasts.

'Got it online,' she said. 'Cool, eh?'

'Very.' He lifted his gaze eventually. 'Well, cheers.'

They clinked glasses and drank. The beer tasted of caramel and chocolate. It was comforting after the madness of Deliverance in his mouth. Adam lifted his glass and looked at the deep ruby colour.

'Very nice,' he said, nodding.

'Told you.'

Adam heard a commotion and turned. Roddy and Ash had stumbled into a nearby table and were apologising and laughing. They pitched up to Adam and Molly, wiping their noses, leaning on each other, eyes like pinpricks. Adam cringed.

'I see you've already met my little sister,' said Molly.

'Hey, Moll,' said Ash, sniffing loudly. 'You know these guys?'

Adam and Roddy stared at the two women, Roddy recovering first.

'Looks like we can skip the introductions,' he said, getting his ridiculous alligator-skin wallet out and riffling the notes stacked inside. 'Why don't you all grab a table and I'll get a round in. It's time to get this party started.'

9

'So you guys are smokeheads?' said Ash, her gaze drifting round the table.

Ethan and Luke had turned up and the six of them were hurtling headlong towards hammered thanks to Roddy's magic porridge pot of a wallet. Drunken noise made a swirling blizzard around them.

'Smokeheads?' said Roddy.

Molly leaned in to the middle of the table. 'It's what we call fans of Islay malts. Outsiders, not the Ileach.'

'The what?' said Ethan.

'Ileach,' said Molly. 'People of Islay. It's Gaelic.'

'Adam's the malt expert,' said Ethan.

'You work in a whisky shop, right?' said Molly, turning to Adam.

Adam sipped his dram, a decent Bunnahabhain but nothing special. 'A tourist trap really, but we have some good stock.'

Roddy had his arm on the back of Ash's seat as he shouted over the table. 'Fuck's sake, you two are made for each other, a distillery guide and a whisky-shop worker. Imagine the little dram-soaked nippers you'd have, suckled on cask strength.'

Adam shifted in his seat. 'Sorry about him,' he said quietly to Molly. 'He's king of the arseholes.'

'Is it him or the coke?' said Molly.

Adam raised his eyebrows, but then realised it was obvious what fuelled Roddy's bullshit. 'Hard to tell them apart, it's been so long since I've seen him without it.'

Molly looked at Roddy whispering in Ash's ear, Ash giggling away. 'I know what you mean, I haven't seen Ash sober in ages.'

Adam looked at Molly, who seemed suddenly downcast.

'Come on,' he said. 'Let's stick some tunes on the jukebox.'

By the time he caught up with her at the ancient, glowing wall-mounted machine she was already punching in numbers off by heart. He flicked through the album covers to find what she'd put on.

'Abba?' he said. 'Seriously?'

Molly smiled in mock offence. 'What's wrong with Abba?'

Adam looked at her. 'Just not my kind of thing, that's all.'

'Don't tell me, landfill indie?'

'What?'

'You know, mortgage rock – Coldplay, Snow Patrol, Editors, all that dreary pish.'

Adam shook his head. 'That's more Roddy's bag.'

The truth was Adam didn't mind that stuff either, but really he'd pretty much given up on music after Britpop and had regressed to his dodgy metal past, digging out old Thin Lizzy, AC/DC and Motörhead albums and sticking them on his cheap iPod imitation.

They walked back to the table. Ash and Roddy had disappeared.

'What did you put on?' Luke drawled. He'd clearly had a few joints back at the B&B.

'Abba,' said Adam, smiling at Molly.

Ethan made a face. 'Not the *Mamma Mia* soundtrack? Debs loves that garbage.'

'Christ no,' said Molly. 'The real deal.'

'Very cool,' said Luke, nodding.

'See?' said Molly, nudging Adam. 'A man after my own heart.'

'I'll leave you to it,' said Adam. 'I need the loo.'

The tiny bogs were rammed so he decided on an al fresco slash, heading out the delivery door to a courtyard stinking of piss and stale beer, lit by a sliver of moon.

As he was about to unzip he spotted two figures in the shadows across the courtyard. He pressed himself into a dark corner.

'Fuck, it's freezing out here,' said the taller of the two. Roddy.

Adam watched as Roddy got something out of his pocket, then heard a loud coke sniff.

'Hey, ladies first,' said the other figure, punching his shoulder. Ash.

He offered up something. She held her hair back, leaned in and snorted. They sniffed and laughed then she kissed him hard, grabbing his crotch.

'Hello,' she said. 'Bad moon rising.'

She knelt and whipped his jeans down in a quick movement. Adam saw her head moving forwards and backwards.

'Fuck,' said Roddy, holding her head in both hands.

Adam watched for a moment then turned back to the pub.

He waited his turn in the urinals, stopping to examine his saggy face in the grubby mirror afterwards. He washed his hands then pulled them still dripping down his face, trying to freshen himself up. He gazed at himself again, then sighed heavily and left.

By the time he got back to the table, Ash and Roddy were sitting there as if nothing had happened, except for a smirk on Roddy's face and a flushed colour in Ash's cheeks.

She took a big swig of JD and turned to Roddy. 'So it's basically your fault the world economy is fucked and we're all skint.'

'We're not *all* skint,' said Roddy, patting his wallet.

Ethan groaned. 'Don't get him started.'

'We're being made scapegoats by the fucking media,' Roddy shouted. 'Fund manager is a job like any other.'

'Except you make millions at the expense of ordinary punters,' said Adam.

'There is that.'

'And get huge bonuses when you succeed, but no punishment when you cock up.'

Roddy beamed. 'I didn't make the rules. And anyway, I don't fuck up, I'm still making pots of money. The best in the business like me are always going to make money. Ask Luke, I got a shit-hot return on his little nest egg.'

Adam turned to Luke. 'Roddy invested for you?'

Luke shrugged.

'Just as a little favour, you understand,' said Roddy. 'I wouldn't normally take on something that small.'

Adam turned to Roddy. 'But people like you have fucked this country's reputation for being good with money.'

'Me?' said Roddy. He pointed at Ethan. 'Take it up with RBS Mortgage Boy over there.'

Ethan shook his head, having none of it. 'You're joking. I design databases, how the hell is it my fault?'

'Your employers managed to work up twenty-four billion in debt, that's not a kick in the arse off the Scottish government's entire budget. White Stone are doing very nicely, thanks, so it's not our fault, is it? It's not about avoiding risk and all that safe, steady shite, it's about knowing which are the right risks to take and taking them.'

Ethan breathed out. 'It's guys like you taking risks and screwing it up that mean we all have to pay in the end.'

'Life's about risks,' said Roddy. 'If you grew up and realised that, maybe you'd be a lot better off than you are now.'

'If you're so rich, Hedge Fund Henry,' Ash slurred, 'why aren't you at the bar getting the fucking drinks in?'

'On my way,' said Roddy with a smug smile.

Ash slid over to Luke.

'So what's your story, quiet boy?' she said.

He examined her with narrow eyes. 'Musician.'

'What do you play?'

'Bit of everything.'

'Drums?'

'Sometimes.'

'I have a thing for drummers. Strong hands and lots of energy.'

She stroked his arm. He looked at Roddy at the bar, then at her hand.

'What are you doing?'

'Flirting, what does it look like?'

'You've spent all night flirting with Roddy.'

'So what?'

59

'Not interested.'

Ash laughed. 'OK, take it easy, Ringo, just being friendly.'

Across the table, Ethan got up to help Roddy with the drinks.

Adam took a deep breath and turned to Molly. Serenity now.

'I couldn't help noticing you're not wearing a wedding ring.'

Molly laughed.

'You couldn't help noticing?' she said, a tease in her voice.

'Actually, Roddy noticed at the distillery.'

'I didn't think I was his type.'

Adam felt sheepish. 'He was looking for me.'

'Was he, now?'

'It's just that you were wearing one last time we met, and you mentioned your husband. Remember, at the Feis Ile?'

Her smile faded. 'A lot's happened since then.'

Her look made him want to rewind. 'I'm sorry, it's none of my business. You obviously don't want to talk about it.'

He put his hand on hers on the table. She shook her head with a resigned look. 'It's not that, it's just . . .'

'Hey,' shouted Roddy, dumping the drinks and sitting down next to Ash. 'It's PC Plod. Evening all.'

Adam followed Roddy's gaze and saw the police officer who'd stopped them earlier standing behind him, looming over their table. He was in a dress shirt and leather jacket, still wearing the gold chain. He looked drunk and itching for trouble.

'Oh, shit,' said Molly, sliding her hand out from under Adam's.

'This should be good,' said Ash.

'Aren't you going to introduce me?' he said to Molly.

'Fuck off.'

He grabbed her arm and gripped firmly. 'I said introduce me.'
'Hey,' said Adam, seeing the look on Molly's face.
She turned to him and sighed deeply.
'Adam, this is my ex-husband, Joe.'

10

'Maybe I should call it a night,' said Molly, looking round.

After some huffing and puffing, Joe had retreated to the other side of the pub where he was chatting to a short weasel with sunken grey eyes and a twitch. Both of them were hammering pints and nips and staring.

'Don't let those pricks get to you,' said Ash. 'They're just a pair of bullies.'

'Who's Gollum with the Bill?' said Roddy loudly.

'Joe's cousin Grant,' said Ash. 'My year at school, total inbred sadsack. Ileach rumour has it that his mum had a thing going with her cousin. She never admitted who his dad was, anyway. Plus, she was on methadone when she had him, and probably shooting up as well. Anywhere else in the country he wouldn't have enough brain cells to snare a job as a fucking toilet attendant. Here on our wonderful island he gets welcomed into the constabulary thanks to family contacts, and gets to act out his snivelling little grudge against the world. He's got no mind of his own, does everything master Joe tells him.'

'That's what passes for law enforcement on the island?' said Adam, shaking his head.

'Pretty much,' said Molly. 'There are a couple of decent cops here, but Joe and Grant treat it like the family business. Joe's dad did it before him for thirty-five years, his grandad before that.'

'They look a right pair of cunts,' said Roddy.

'Correct,' said Ash.

Molly glugged at her pint.

'You OK?' said Adam.

She slurped, trying to get through her drink. 'I really think it's best if I go home.'

'Stay for a bit, Moll,' said Ash. 'If you leave, you're letting them win.'

'I don't need the hassle.'

Roddy puffed his chest out, sensing a damsel in distress. 'What's Joe's problem anyway?'

Molly sighed heavily. 'It's a long story.'

Ash was agitated and fidgeting. 'Sis, you've got nothing to feel bad about.'

'I know that.'

'I'm not sure you do.'

'It's not as simple as you think.'

Ash's eyes widened. 'I hope to fuck you're not making excuses for that bastard.'

'Of course not. You know how I feel about him.'

'It doesn't matter what happened to him, the way he treated you was unforgivable.'

'I know that, it's just . . .'

'What do you mean?' said Roddy.

Ash's mouth was running off. 'Joe gave her this big sob story for years . . .'

'Ash, please . . .' Molly said, but Ash had a tailwind.

'All the Ileach thought his dad was this pillar of the community, a friendly copper and upstanding member of society, all the while he was beating seven shades of shite out of Joe and his mum behind their front door.'

'Can we change the subject?' said Molly.

'Then once Joe left home and joined the force in some perverted attempt to please his twat of a dad, his mum killed herself, threw herself over the side of the ferry one night on the way to the mainland. That's the story anyway. Joe lost it, basically, turned into a total nutcase. Round about then his dad keeled over from a massive coronary. Just as well because I reckon Joe was about to do the job for him.'

Molly looked nervously over at Joe and Grant. 'I'm sure the guys don't want to hear all this crap.'

Ash couldn't be stopped. 'But none of that matters a fuck, it's no excuse for what he did to you.'

'What did he do?' said Roddy.

'Ash, that's enough.' Molly gave her an evil glare, which finally seemed to get through.

'I'm just saying he's a total arsehole,' said Ash. 'And all the domestic abuse in the world isn't an excuse for that.'

'Don't worry,' Roddy said to Molly. 'We'll look after you. Stay.'

Molly laughed bitterly. 'You've no idea.'

She finished her beer, stood up and put her coat on, fumbling with her arms in the sleeves.

'Wait,' said Adam, reaching for her. 'If you're definitely going, at least let me walk you home.'

She looked at Adam, then at Joe. 'I don't know.'

'Please.'

She sighed. 'OK, whatever. Let's just get out of here.'

Adam downed his whisky and pulled his coat on. They

said goodbye and made their way through the crowded bar, Molly leading. A few feet from the door, Joe appeared and grabbed her arm.

'Leaving so soon?'

Molly tried to shrug him off, but he had a tight hold.

'Let go,' she said. 'I'm going home.'

Joe looked at Adam and laughed. 'With him? Fuck me, your standards have slipped.'

'Let go of her,' said Adam, his pulse pounding in his throat.

Joe laughed again. 'Or what?'

'Or I'll make you.'

'Just leave it,' said Molly, struggling.

'Did you hear that, Grantie?' said Joe as his short-arsed mate appeared next to him.

'Yeah,' said Grant, his eyes darting back and forth, the tip of his tongue stuck between his teeth.

'This cunt wants some action.'

'Why don't you just leave us alone?' said Adam.

'You come into my local and leave with my wife and expect me to hold the fucking door for you?'

'*Ex*-wife,' said Molly.

'What's the problem here?' It was Roddy at Adam's side.

'It's OK, I'm handling it,' said Adam.

Joe laughed sarcastically. 'It's OK, he's handling it, so fuck off.'

'Sounds like you need a lesson in manners,' said Roddy.

'Oh, for fuck's sake,' said Joe, rolling his eyes. 'Listen to college boy.'

He released Molly's arm, then in a swift movement punched both Roddy and Adam square in the face, buckling

66

them over. He kneed Adam under the chin, knocking him off his feet, then rained punches down on the back of Roddy's head, Molly grabbing his arm but failing to stop the blows.

Luke arrived and shoved Joe off balance, enough for Ethan to pull Roddy out of reach. Adam looked up and shuffled backwards as Molly and Ash helped him up. Joe and Grant glared at them.

'You lot, out.' It was the barman, pointing at Adam and the rest.

'He started it,' said Roddy, holding his nose.

The barman was nonplussed. 'Doesn't matter. I want you out.'

'You can't bar me,' said Ash. 'I fucking work here.'

'You and Molly can stay, those four are leaving.'

'Fuck's sake,' said Adam, wheezing and rubbing his chin.

'Let's just go,' said Molly, leading Adam to the door.

The whole pub watched.

'Run along now,' Joe hissed between his teeth, fists clenched at his side.

As Roddy passed, Joe dummied a headbutt, sniggering as Roddy flinched.

'You better hope I never see you cunts again,' said Joe. 'I won't go so easy on you next time.'

II

'Well, this is me.'

Adam's heart sank. They'd only walked a couple of minutes; he wanted more time with her. They stood outside a small brownstone terraced house on the Back Road behind the bay, Gillespie nameplate on the door. The others had gone back to the B&B where Roddy had more coke and three bottles of Ardbeg single cask stashed. Adam grimaced as he fingered the two Viagra that Roddy had slipped into his pocket.

Molly smiled. 'How's the nose?'

'Just a scratch,' he said, raising a hand to it.

'It's still bleeding,' she said. 'Christ, I'm sorry.'

'It's not your fault.'

'Yes it is, I married the arsehole.'

Adam laughed and a bubble of snotty blood popped from his nose. 'Aw, shit.'

'You'd better come in till that stops bleeding.'

'It's fine.'

Molly fished keys out of her bag and opened the door.

'Come on,' she nodded inside. 'I've got a thirty-year-old sherry-butt Laphroaig needs drinking.'

'Ninety-seven bottling?'

'The very same.'

'Well, in that case.'

He followed her to the living room and she fetched the

whisky. The decor was old-fashioned, patterned wallpaper, saggy sofas, mahogany display cabinets. There were framed pictures of Molly and Ash as kids, then as young women smiling with an old couple.

'Mum and Dad,' said Molly, handing him a glass of dark amber.

'This their house?'

'It was,' said Molly, touching the picture. 'They're dead.'

'Shit, sorry.'

Molly shrugged. 'Mum got cancer two years ago. At least it was quick. Six weeks after diagnosis she was gone.'

Adam shifted awkwardly.

'Dad drank himself to death not long after,' said Molly. 'Easy to do on this island. They found him on the beach one morning after a skinful.'

'Christ, Molly, I'm so sorry.'

'You've nothing to feel sorry about.' She looked at him. 'Your folks still alive, then?'

'My dad is, my mum died from a stroke ten years ago.'

He felt a tingle as she touched his arm, and thought about the last time he'd seen his dad. Christmas lunch just the two of them, his wee sister unable to make it back from whatever glamorous shit she was up to in Los Angeles. Without his mum there, Christmas was just silence and sadness, a reminder of what was missing as well as a glimpse into his own future, a string of lonely meals into old age.

Molly sat on one of the sofas and motioned for him to join her.

'Still, at least my folks dying gave me the kick up the arse to leave Joe,' she said. 'Ash was still living here with them and she

70

lost the plot. I had to look after her. I had an excuse to get out.'

She sipped and Adam did likewise.

'What do you think?' she said, nodding at his glass.

'Very fresh,' he said. 'I get lemon, rosewater and almonds amongst the seaweed and smoke.' He paused. 'The finish has great balance.'

'Doesn't it? I'm sure I get some heather and coffee in there too.'

Adam took another sip. 'Yeah, I can see that. Like coffee-flavoured chocolates or something.'

'Exactly.' Molly smiled and looked at her glass. 'You realise this whisky is older than we are? That's kind of incredible to think about, isn't it?'

'It is.'

She looked at the picture of her parents then got up and opened a door on the cabinet to reveal an old turntable. She lifted an album from alongside and put it on, lazy jazz emerging.

'My dad's records,' she said. 'This is Charlie Parker and Dizzy Gillespie. I'm sure half the reason he liked Dizzy was because we had the same surname. He used to call me "Little Dizzy" when I was wee.'

'You must miss them a lot.'

Molly sat down. 'I've had plenty of other shit on my plate. The divorce, looking after Ash. Sometimes it feels like I've never really had time to mourn.'

There was silence between them, washed by flowing trumpet lines.

'I know what you're thinking,' she said after a while. 'How the hell did I get hooked up with a bastard like Joe?'

71

Adam shook his head.

'I wonder myself, every day,' she said. 'But he wasn't always like he is now. He was sweet and caring in the beginning, full of ideas and energy. All that stuff Ash said in the pub about his dad was true, but he never seemed affected by it initially, never let it get him down. We used to stay up all night making plans. This sounds stupid now, but we used to have this crazy idea about starting up our own distillery, fixing up one of the old disused places and running it as a small family business.'

Adam felt his pulse race as his hand came up to check the papers in his jacket pocket.

'That doesn't sound stupid at all,' he said, trying to keep his voice level.

'But somehow all those dreams faded.' Molly sighed and looked up. 'You don't want to hear all this.'

Adam wanted to keep her talking so that he could keep looking in her beautiful eyes. 'I don't mind.'

'When he joined the police, that was the start of it.' Molly was whispering now. 'He didn't want to follow his dad originally, but he couldn't get decent work anywhere else, and the force was great pay and conditions. I tried to talk him out of it, but he joined anyway. Somehow he gradually became hard, like his dad, as if it was a competition. Eventually we got to the stage where we never talked about plans or dreams any more. When his mum died, he shut me out, this big macho thing about taking the pain on his own.'

Adam swallowed heavily. 'What did Ash mean about the way he treated you?'

Molly hesitated and looked away.

'Forget I asked,' said Adam.

'No, it's OK,' she said. 'We tried to have kids, but it didn't go well. I had three miscarriages.'

'Christ, Molly.'

She shrugged. 'Happens all the time, it's much more common than you think. But Joe didn't take it well, he blamed me. He drank a lot and started getting abusive. Shouting and screaming at first, then . . .'

Adam reached for her hand but she pulled it away. He didn't know what to say or do, so he just raised his glass and sipped.

'Anyway, it's all in the past now,' she said, looking round and taking a deep breath. She waved an arm. 'So this is where me and Ash live.'

'You don't seem to have much in common with her.'

'She's changed a lot since Mum and Dad died.'

'You lost your parents too.'

'It's harder for her, she's eight years younger than me. I have to look out for her. She used to make jewellery, you know, beautiful silverware. She was going to set up her own company. Now she just works in the pub, drinks herself stupid every night and fucks whoever's in front of her.'

'And what about you?'

'You mean who do I fuck?'

'Shit, that's not what I meant at all,' he said, flustered.

'I'm winding you up.'

'Thanks. I meant what do you want to do with your life?'

'As opposed to being a shitty little tour guide?'

'No, no, working at Laphroaig is great, I just mean . . .'

'You're quite easy to wind up.'

Adam pressed the button on his watch and sneaked a look.

'You leaving?' said Molly.

'I wasn't looking at the time.'

'Then what?'

He sighed. 'My watch has a heart-rate monitor on it.'

'Really?' she said, holding his wrist for a better look. 'What's the damage?'

'105 bpm.'

'Holy shit, are you an alien or something?'

'Very funny.'

'I mean it,' she laughed, placing a hand on his chest. 'Are you running the hundred metres in there?'

He liked the feel of her touch, could smell her perfume mingling with the fumes from his whisky glass. She let go of him and sipped her dram.

'Actually, I'm taking night classes at Bowmore High,' she said.

'Yeah?'

'Chemistry and maths. Never did much school first time round. Working at the distillery, though, I realised I've got a pretty good palate. I figured maybe in the long run I could do chemistry at uni and try for a job with one of the big drinks guys, or even better as a stillman or master distiller.'

'That would be amazing.'

'It's a pipedream.'

'I think you'd be fantastic at it. Like you say, you've got a beautiful palate.'

'I bet you say that to all the girls.' She smiled then shrugged. 'My dad worked in the warehouse at Lagavulin his whole life, had to retire when he knackered his hip. He would be so proud if I managed to make something of myself.'

'I'm sure he'd be proud of you no matter what you do.'

'Maybe.' She sipped her whisky. 'You know in the old days

they used to hand out several drams a day to all distillery staff, to stop them stealing bigger amounts of the stuff? Cask strength, too. My dad got pissed every day at work for thirty years.'

Adam nodded. He'd heard the stories, but never really believed them.

'They basically created an island full of alcoholics,' said Molly, shaking her head.

There was silence for a moment.

'So what about you?' she said.

'You mean, am I an alcoholic?'

Molly smiled. 'No, I mean do you want to work in a whisky shop your whole life?'

Adam felt his heart thud against his ribs. 'Actually, I have big plans.'

'Do tell.'

'You'll laugh.'

'Try me.'

'It's quite a coincidence, really, considering what you were just talking about.'

'You're going to become an alcoholic?'

'Not exactly.'

'Come on, out with it.'

He took a deep breath and reached into his pocket. He pulled out creased papers, plans and photos and began to unfold them in front of her.

'I want to open a distillery here on Islay.'

12

Molly raised her eyebrows but didn't speak, which Adam took as a cue to crack on.

'There's a derelict farmhouse distillery out at Stremnishmore, you know it?'

'On the Oa?'

Adam nodded.

'Heard of it, never been there, though. It's pretty remote out that way.'

'It's perfect,' said Adam, spreading everything out on the sofa between them. 'I went to see it last time I was on the island, a lot of the equipment is still in decent condition. The owners are happy to sell. It still has a water supply from Loch Kinnabus, everything's in place to get it going again. I've had a business plan put together and some quotes, reckon I can get the whole thing operational for a million pounds.'

Molly shuffled through the papers and photos, smiled and sipped. 'Where are you going to get that kind of money?'

Adam looked down at his drink. 'That's why I'm here this weekend. I'm going to ask Roddy.'

'Why bring him all the way here to ask?'

Adam looked up. 'I just thought if he saw it he'd understand. He's never been to Islay before. I hoped he'd get caught up in the spirit of the place.'

Molly looked through the stuff Adam had given her.

'Do you think he'll go for it?' she asked.

Adam nodded. 'It's a good investment. There's a growing market for Islay malts, even with the recession. Look at Bruichladdich and Kilchoman. Small boutique operations are springing up all over the place. This would be the only distillery on the Oa, with a distinct character all its own. I know enough about the whisky industry to market it properly. Obviously I'd need to employ the right people, but there's lots of industry experience here on the island, I'm sure that wouldn't be a problem. I could even hire you.'

'Getting carried away a wee bit, aren't you? Shouldn't you wait to see what he says?'

'I think he'll go for it, I really do. It's not as if he doesn't have the money.'

'When are you going to ask?'

'I've planned a surprise trip to the site tomorrow morning. Want to come?'

'I wouldn't want to get in the way.'

'Not at all, having you there might help, knowing the locals are on board and all that.'

Molly looked doubtful.

'You do think it's a good idea, don't you?' said Adam.

Molly sifted through the paperwork and finished her whisky before answering. 'I think it's a great idea. I mean, I dreamed about doing something like this with Joe for years. But there's so much to consider. It won't be as easy as you think.'

'I know it's going to be hard work, but I really think I can make a go of it.'

Molly reached for the bottle and refilled their glasses.

'Good luck.'

'So you'll come tomorrow?'

She looked him in the eye. 'Sure, why not?'

Adam grinned and raised his glass. 'Here's to the Oa single malt, available in all good whisky shops in ten years' time.'

They clinked glasses and sipped, the ancient smoke filling their chests. Eventually Molly spoke.

'So, how did you get into whisky in the first place? I was brought up on Islay; what's your excuse?'

'My dad,' said Adam. 'He never really had extravagant tastes in anything else, but he always had a decent bottle of malt in the house. He used to work as an engineer at the local power station. I remember he would come in after a shift all hangdog and knackered, and the first thing he did was pour himself a stiff one. The change that came over him when he smelt that spirit then tasted it was amazing, like the weight of the world was lifted from his shoulders. It wasn't about the alcohol, he didn't have a drink problem or anything, he just loved what whisky represented, the release from the humdrum world of work into something more, I don't know, spiritual, I guess, if you'll excuse the pun.'

'That's probably the nicest thing anyone's ever said about their dad needing a drink to face his family,' said Molly, grinning.

Adam laughed. 'It wasn't like that at all. He wasn't drinking to forget, he was drinking to remember, to remember the beautiful complexity of the world, to treat himself to a glimpse of what the big wide world was like.'

'And to get pissed.'

'OK, and to get pissed.' Adam raised his glass and drank.

'He took me to the Scotch Malt Whisky Society on my eighteenth birthday. I'd been getting steaming for years before that on cheap lager and cider, but this was a revelation. We had umpteen single-cask Islay malts that night, and I felt like pulling up trees and climbing mountains, the buzz was completely different to getting hammered with my mates.'

'What is it about Islay malts that are so special?'

'You have to ask?'

Molly shrugged. 'I've grown up around them, it's hard for me to have any perspective. I've always wondered what drives smokeheads.'

'It's the combination of everything. The Islay malts feel so Scottish, yet totally international at the same time, more so than other whiskies.' He raised his glass and looked at it. 'This liquid is older than us, and its incredible flavours are a combination of a million different factors, from the seaweed next to the Laphroaig warehouse to the Spanish oak of the butts, from the peat smoke of the furnaces to the sherry that was stored in the barrel before it. No other drink borrows so much from outside influences, really absorbs those tastes and flavours and sensations then transforms them into something utterly new and original. I think the whole process is amazing.'

She was sitting closer to him now, his plans and papers fallen onto the floor. He found himself staring into her big green eyes, then suddenly somehow he was locked in an awkward and tentative kiss, tasting the smoke on her tongue and the sweetness of her lipstick, feeling the softness of her hair in his hand. How had that happened?

After a few moments she pulled away and placed a hand on his face.

'Let's just take it easy,' she said. 'You seem like a nice guy, but . . .'

He held her hand. 'It's OK.'

She smiled and Adam felt a burning in his chest, a swirling blend of happiness and old spirit.

13

He woke with the taste of peat in his mouth. He was on Molly's sofa under a blanket, watery light rippling through the window. His watch on the coffee table said 8:45 a.m. Next to it was the empty Laphroaig bottle, two sticky tumblers and a note.

Had to nip to work for a bit. See you at your B&B later for the big trip? Thanks for last night, Moll x

He remembered the kiss. He ran a finger along his lips then licked it. The faint fizzy film of her lipstick was still there. They'd stayed up for hours talking about his plans for the distillery, her idea of going to uni, swapping whisky anecdotes. He couldn't remember when they'd gone to sleep, or how the night ended.

He pulled the blanket off. He was fully dressed apart from his shoes, which were neatly arranged under the coffee table. As he pulled them on he heard the front door open, then Ash came in, dishevelled and bleary.

She smiled when she saw him. 'Aye-aye, dirty stop-out.'

'Look who's talking.'

'Touché.' She threw her coat on the floor and left the room, returning with a carton of orange juice. 'Where's Moll?'

'Gone to work,' said Adam, folding the note and putting it in his pocket.

She took a big swig from the carton. 'You two get it on last night?'

Adam stood up, felt his head pound. 'None of your business.'

'I'll take that as a no.' She narrowed her eyes. 'Listen, just be careful, OK? She's been through a fuck of a lot lately, and I don't want you adding to her grief.'

'I don't intend to.'

'I swear to God, if you upset her, I'll rip your bollocks off and feed them to you.'

'I love you, too.'

'I mean it. You've no idea what she put up with from that wanker.'

'I have some idea.'

'No, you don't. He used to hit her, and worse. Much worse. If you tell her I told you, it'll be bollocks-on-a-plate time, you got me?'

'Loud and clear.'

'Good. I'm off to bed.' She ran a hand through her straggly hair. 'Tell Roddy if he wants to find me, I'm working in the Ardview tonight.'

'We're barred, remember?'

'Oh yeah. Well, whatever.'

She left the room and Adam looked around for his jacket, pulling it on and heading out the door.

Outside it was a shivering, clear morning. Seaweed and brine smacked him in the face as he walked back to the B&B. He thought about what Ash said. Worse than beating your wife meant one thing, and his stomach knotted at the thought of it.

He remembered the punch from Joe then the feel of

Molly's lips, then tried to shake his mind clear to think about today. This morning was his big chance to persuade Roddy, to turn his life around, and here he was hungover and thinking about her.

He was on the beach now, plastic junk littering the sand. He could smell diesel and rotting fish mixed with the salty air and residual whisky fumes in his nose. He spotted Ethan leaning against a low wall outside the B&B, putting his mobile away.

'How's Debs?'

Ethan looked up and frowned. He seemed to size Adam up then decide something. 'Not great, actually.'

'No?'

Ethan sighed. 'I never told you guys, but we've started IVF.'

'Really?'

'Three years we were trying for kids, no joy. All the tests came back fine, but it just wasn't happening. It's been frustrating.'

'I can imagine.'

Ethan looked up. 'With all due respect, I don't think you can. Anyway, we started treatment, but she's just found out the first cycle didn't work.'

'Shit, Ethan, I'm sorry.'

Ethan rubbed his temple and squeezed his eyes tight. 'Two grand down the toilet, and we need to wait months to try again.'

'Two grand?'

Ethan raised his eyebrows. 'I know. I wouldn't care about the money, but the shit's hitting the fan at work as well.'

'Yeah?'

He gave Adam a tired look. 'You know what it's like at the moment, RBS are all over the fucking news. They're sacking nine thousand staff, you think that won't affect us?'

'I presumed you were safe.'

'No one's safe. Chat is that half our department is getting the chop. Chances are either me or Debs will get the bullet. Maybe both.'

'Jesus, I had no idea.'

Ethan shook his head. 'That's because I don't shoot my mouth off all day like some people we know. Honestly, Roddy's got a real cheek having a pop at me last night about money and risks. It's because of morons like him that me and Debs are in this mess. If either of us gets sacked, we're screwed. Can't pay the mortgage or the car loan, and we just wasted two thousand quid on some useless eggs.'

'I'm sorry, Ethan, I really am.'

'The stress won't be helping Debs, either. She's taking it all pretty badly. Maybe I should just head home.'

Adam shook his head. 'You're here now, you might as well try and make the most of it. Could be your last jolly in a while. You'll be home by tomorrow night anyway. Would it really make that much difference to get back a day early?'

'I suppose you're right.' Ethan took a deep breath and tried to smile. 'So, I take it you've been at Molly's all night?'

Adam made a noncommittal face.

'She seems nice,' said Ethan.

'She is.'

'That sister of hers is a loose cannon.'

'Yeah, I just saw her,' said Adam. 'She threatened to rip my balls off.'

'Sounded through the wall like she was doing that to Roddy all night.' Ethan laughed then looked at Adam.

'What about Molly's ex?'

'What about him?'

'He's a piece of work.'

'Yeah.'

'Can't believe we got barred from the only decent pub in town on our first night.'

'That's what happens if you fight a copper.'

'He started it.'

Adam shrugged, the Clash song going through his head. They stood in silence, gulls gliding on thermals high overhead. Eventually Ethan spoke.

'I know you all take the mick out of me for being a boring sod,' he said. 'Always checking in with the missus.'

'We don't.'

'Come on, I'm not a bloody idiot. Just because I'm married and settled doesn't mean I'm not the same person you were at uni with.'

'I know that.'

'It's just that my priorities have changed, you know?'

'Ethan, who the hell are we to take the piss out of you? You've got a proper, grown-up life, we're all still dicking around like teenagers.'

More silence as the sun disappeared in a distant grey haze.

'So what are we doing today?' said Ethan after a while.

Adam looked at him. 'I've got something special planned.'

'Oh yeah?'

14

'Take it easy,' said Adam, hand braced against the glove compartment.

They were bumping over a rough single-track in the Audi, Roddy tanning it too fast over summits and round blind corners. If they met something coming the other way they were screwed. Molly was nestled between Luke and Ethan in the back, Snow Patrol blaring out of the speakers.

Roddy laughed. 'I'll slow down if you tell me where the fuck we're going.'

Adam looked at him. 'We're nearly there.'

'What's the big fucking mystery?'

'You'll see soon enough.'

Adam looked at his watch. He pressed the button – 102 bpm. He took deep breaths and looked out the window. At least the weather was decent, clear cobalt skies above, just a murky grey cloudbank miles away to the west. It would hopefully show the distillery buildings in a good light. He felt his palm sweaty against the glove compartment and lifted it to see red lines where he'd been pressing. The car swung round a corner and he reached forward again. His other hand patted his jacket pocket, checking yet again that the business plans were still there. Serenity now.

They came over a rise and spotted a huge stone tower in the distance.

'What's the giant cock?' said Roddy.

'American Monument,' said Molly, leaning forward.

'What?'

'Built to commemorate the people who died when an American ship was torpedoed by a German sub off the coast in 1918.'

'And they thought a massive bell-end was appropriate?'

'It's supposed to look like a lighthouse.'

They drove on, glimpses of dark moorland on either side, peat bog then heather and bracken, rough, unwelcoming terrain all around.

Ethan struggled to unfold an OS map. 'Where exactly are we?'

'On the Oa,' said Molly.

'The what?'

'The Oa.'

'It sounds like you're saying "The Oh".'

Molly laughed. 'I am.'

'How do you spell it?'

'O, A. Oa. The Oa.'

'Oh, the Oa,' said Ethan, smiling. He peered out the window. 'Not much sign of life on the Oa.'

'It's the island's most remote peninsula,' said Molly. 'Thousands used to live here, forced out in the Clearances.'

They passed a ruined farm, rough stone gable ends still standing, roof long since collapsed. Black-faced sheep chewed at grass tufts on both sides of the crumbled walls.

'Apparently there are two whole abandoned villages on the Oa,' said Molly. 'Although I've never seen them. You can't get to them by road.'

'Does anyone still live out here?' said Ethan.

'A few farms, that's about it.'

'So where are we going?'

Molly looked at her lap.

'You know, don't you?' said Ethan.

She shrugged.

'Illicit still?' drawled Luke.

'What?'

'All this wilderness, man, perfect peace and quiet for making peatreek, yeah?'

Molly laughed and shook her head. 'Not any more, I don't think. Used to be loads of bootlegging all over the island, but not for a long time.'

'Why not?'

Molly lifted her shoulders.

'Maybe nobody's got the balls,' said Roddy, changing up through the gears.

Molly and Adam shared a glance. Adam started to feel queasy as they got closer to their destination.

'Buzzard,' said Luke, eyes skywards.

A large brown bird was gliding high over a cliff, charcoal sea spraying against ragged rocks below.

Molly nodded. 'A lot of the Oa is an RSPB reserve. There are golden eagles at the American Monument somewhere, but I've never spotted them.'

Luke raised his eyebrows.

'Don't get twitcher going,' laughed Roddy. 'He'll spunk his pants if he sees golden fucking eagles.'

The car horn blared, making them all jump, then they braked sharply.

'Fucking stupid sheep,' shouted Roddy as a large ram sauntered off the track and onto the verge, wiggling its woolly arse in defiance.

The track got rougher, potholes and rocks scattered all over, no more passing places. To their left was a steep cliff down to the sea, on the right they passed the ruins of an old church, moss-covered gravestones jerking out at odd angles.

'This really is the arse-end of nowheresville,' said Roddy, looking out the window.

'This is it,' said Adam as they came over a blind summit and saw a spread of low grey buildings at the end of the road.

15

'What the fuck are we supposed to be seeing?' said Roddy getting out of the car.

A straggle of tired buildings was strung in a crescent facing the muddy clearing where they'd parked. Paint peeled from window frames and doors and the whitewash was filthy grey from the battering of the elements.

'Potential,' said Adam. 'Follow me.'

He walked towards the nearest of the buildings, digging keys out of his pocket. He undid a padlock and opened the old wooden door.

'Come on,' he said, ducking inside.

The rest of them looked at each other then followed.

Inside, Adam stood next to a table strewn with bits of paper. Behind him were three large copper stills linked by a gantry and metal stairs, the familiar witch's-hat shapes linked by tarnished pipes. The floor was covered in birdshit and bits of masonry, and as they entered a pigeon made a flustered flap into the rafters. Thin light through a high window picked out dust dancing in the air.

'Well,' said Adam. 'What do you think?'

'I think you've brought us to a shithole at the end of the world,' said Roddy.

'It's a disused distillery,' said Ethan. 'So what?'

Luke's eyes lit up. 'An illegal still, man.'

Adam smiled. 'There will be nothing illegal about it. This is Stremnishmore distillery. I plan to buy it, renovate it and turn it into a working proposition again. I'm going to make whisky. I've got it all worked out, look.'

He waved excitedly at the plans, bills and forms on the table.

'The owners have agreed to sell me the place and I've got quotes for the renovation work, licence agreements sorted, the lot. I've even got suppliers and distributors lined up, plus a handful of possible employees from the island.'

'You're serious,' said Ethan.

'Deadly,' said Adam. 'This is the big chance to do something with my life. You all know how passionate I am about whisky. This is my chance to actually do something about it instead of rotting in that stupid shop forever.'

'Cool,' said Luke, nodding.

Roddy was shaking his head and grinning. 'You're going to own and run your own distillery?'

Adam looked at him and took a breath.

'I was kind of hoping we would own it together.'

'What?'

'Wouldn't it be amazing?' said Adam. 'Imagine our bottles sitting next to Laphroaig and Ardbeg in the Islay section of whisky shops.'

Roddy narrowed his eyes. 'How much?'

'What?'

'I presume you're asking me to invest in this pipedream, so cut the bullshit and tell me how much.'

'The thing is . . .'

'Just give me a figure.' There was a steeliness in Roddy's

voice Adam hadn't heard before. He didn't like it.

'With start-up costs and wages for the first few years factored in, given that we can't sell the product until . . .'

'A number, please.'

'One point two million would cover it.'

Roddy threw his head back for show and laughed.

'It wouldn't be as much as that to begin with,' said Adam hurriedly. 'We could start online sales of the new spirit after a year, and we could even bring in some money from a visitor centre and cafe, maybe run whisky-making courses in the quiet season, other distilleries . . .'

'You mean it, don't you?' said Roddy. 'You actually want me to give you over a million fucking quid . . .'

'Not *give* it to me, invest it in this place. Roddy, it's a great opportunity. You know yourself that the whisky industry has been bulletproof during the credit crunch, in fact the market for Islay malts is going through the roof in the Far East and India . . .'

'Go to a fucking bank.'

'What?'

'I said go to a bank. Loaning people money is what they do.'

'Come on, Roddy . . .'

'Go to the bank.'

'I already went to the bank.'

'And?'

'What do you think? I don't have a track record in the industry, I'm not a successful businessman, I didn't have any collateral to borrow against. They weren't going to give me a million quid.'

'So why should I?'

Adam felt his heart thudding against his ribcage.

'Because you know me,' he pleaded. 'We've been friends for twenty fucking years. I've never asked you for anything in all that time, but I'm asking you now. It's not a favour, it's a sound investment.'

'What makes you think I have that kind of money lying around?'

'Come on, you're always talking about how much you make.' Adam heard his voice rise in pitch but couldn't control it. 'This is probably peanuts to you, you make this much in yearly bonuses.'

'That might be true, but I didn't get to be the best in the business by throwing money at pie-in-the-sky projects.'

'It's not pie in the sky,' said Adam, panicking. 'If you'll just take a look at the business plan, the figures all stack up. You can have whatever percentage of the company you like, I'm just interested in making quality whisky.'

'This isn't *Dragon's* fucking *Den*,' laughed Roddy. 'We're talking about a million quid and change of my money getting pished into a big black hole at the end of a dirt track on a God-forsaken rock in the Atlantic. It's not going to happen.'

Molly piped up. 'You could at least take a look at the details of the proposal, Roddy. It seems like Adam's gone to a lot of work putting this together.'

Roddy turned and stared. 'He's got you in his corner, has he? Well listen, darling, I don't need to take a look at the details, because I'm not going to throw money away on a ridiculous scheme like this.'

'It could work,' said Molly. 'Bruichladdich have proved

that. And there's a new farmhouse distillery at Kilchoman that's doing great business already after only three years.'

'That's right,' said Adam, feeling sweat on his hands. 'I've arranged for us to have a chat with the owner and manager of Kilchoman this afternoon, take a look round the place. It's amazing what they've done in such a short time.'

'You're wasting your time,' said Roddy. 'I'm not investing in this fucking crazy idea.'

'But why not?' Adam begged.

Roddy stared hard. 'Because, Adam, you're one of life's losers, you always have been and you always will be. You're almost forty and still working in a shop, for fuck's sake. You've spent your whole life being petrified of taking a chance on anything. That doesn't necessarily make you a bad person, but it sure as shit doesn't make you the kind of person who runs a successful business either. You never take risks, it's that simple, so you'll always be one of the also-rans. You're a beta male through and through.'

'But don't you see, I'm trying to change that with this project,' Adam said. 'I'm trying to turn things round, take risks and grab life by the bollocks.'

Roddy smiled. 'Did you fuck Molly last night?'

'What?'

'I said did you fuck her?'

'Mind your own business,' said Molly.

Adam looked confused. 'What's that got to do with anything?'

Roddy shook his head. 'Man, you couldn't get laid if you fell into a barrel of fannies. You can't even pull with a woman who actually likes you, that's how much of a risk-taker you are. I bet you've still got those two Viagras I gave you.'

Adam looked at Molly. 'I didn't want them, he put them in my pocket and . . .' He turned back to Roddy. 'Anyway, that's got nothing to do with anything. This is business we're talking about.'

'It's all part of life's rich tapestry,' said Roddy. 'Loser in love, loser in life.'

Adam was exasperated. 'Look, at least consider it,' he said, picking up the paperwork and thrusting it at Roddy. 'Take a look at the numbers and the plans, and if you don't like it, then fair enough.'

'I don't need to, I'm not investing.' Roddy walked towards the door, kicking up dirt.

'Fuck's sake,' said Adam, grabbing his coat. 'If you were a friend, you'd at least consider it.'

Roddy turned sharply, grabbed Adam and shoved him against a wall, pinning him. 'If you were a friend, you wouldn't ask me to pish away a million quid of my own money on a no-hope fucking joke of a scheme.'

He released Adam in a cloud of masonry dust and turned. 'Right, I'm getting in the car and driving away from this shitheap. If you lot want a lift back to civilisation, I suggest you're in the car in two minutes.'

He swept out of the stillroom, leaving Adam scrambling around picking up the plans that had scattered on the filthy floor.

'Fucking hell,' he said.

The others helped him collect up the paperwork.

'I guess that didn't go according to plan,' said Ethan

quietly as he and Luke headed towards the door.

Molly put an arm round Adam and led him out of the stillroom.

'Don't give up just yet,' she said.

16

Bad feeling hung in the car. Roddy pushed buttons on the stereo.

'Fucking cheap shite,' he growled. 'Piece of crap bollocks.'

He got out a hipflask, took a swig and passed it to Luke, sitting impassively next to him. Ethan was wedged between Molly and a forlorn Adam in the back. The Oa sped past outside, a rough blur of greens and browns. Behind them, heavy clouds were roiling over the ocean.

'I know what you're all thinking,' Roddy shouted. 'I'm the bad guy here. Well, fuck that. We're talking about over a million fucking quid. If it's such a great idea, why doesn't one of you invest in his little plan, eh? See how you like it?'

He drove one-handed, reaching into a pocket for his coke case. He flipped it out, tapped a line onto his steering hand and snorted. The car swerved round a bend too fast then he regained control.

'Easy, man,' said Luke, passing the hipflask into the back. Ethan and Molly passed. Adam took it and stared at Roddy.

'You think I can't see you glaring at me?' said Roddy into the rear-view mirror. 'The silent treatment is schoolboy stuff, give it a fucking rest.'

'Why don't you give it a rest,' said Adam quietly.

'What?'

'You haven't shut up since we got to Islay. You're a big

coked-up bullshit machine, running on the sound of your own voice.'

'Fuck you, dipshit.'

'I think we all need to calm down,' said Ethan. 'Why don't we just pretend this little outing never happened, OK?'

'It's not as simple as that,' said Adam, taking a big swig from the flask.

'Guess what you're drinking,' said Roddy, laughing.

'Go to hell,' Adam snarled.

'Go on, you know you want to.'

Furious as he was, Adam still couldn't resist the challenge. He took a sniff then a sip. Hard to taste straight from the flask, pewter and polish contaminating the palate, but he got a massive raw boot of peat, at least 40 ppm, followed by green apples and mint, then syrup and raisins. It was impressive. Young and a bit showy, but huge body. He'd never tasted it before, but the gimmicky flavours suggested the one distillery where they were always dicking around with new expressions.

'Bruichladdich,' he said.

'Go on.'

'Peaty, but not enough to be the Octomore,' he said. 'A Port Charlotte?'

'Which one?'

'PC6?'

Roddy tilted his head. 'I don't know how you do it, it's a fucking gift.'

'Don't patronise me, you fathead prick.'

'I was paying you a fucking compliment.'

Adam chucked the flask into Roddy's lap. 'If you think I'm such a bloody expert, why don't you put your money where your mouth is and back me up?'

'There's a big difference between telling Caol Ila from Lagavulin and running your own business, trust me.'

'I wouldn't trust you as far as I could throw you.'

'What's that supposed to mean?'

'You're nothing but a self-centred jerk-off, looking out for number one.'

'Of course I am, you're the same, everyone is,' said Roddy, glancing back. 'The difference is, at least I'm fucking honest about it.'

'I'm nothing like you,' said Adam.

'Yeah, you're a fucking hypocrite,' said Roddy. 'You're only upset because you didn't get your own way back at the distillery. You've always been like that, a spoilt little arsehole with delusions of moral superiority.'

Adam was surprised to see his own fist moving fast towards the front of the car, clumsily catching Roddy on the side of the head somewhere behind his left ear.

'Shit,' said Roddy jerking forward and making the car lurch. 'What the fuck?'

He looked round and swung his left arm wildly behind him, missing Adam but catching Ethan on the nose.

'Ow,' said Ethan, holding his hands to his face.

'Jesus . . .' said Molly.

'Watch out, man,' shouted Luke, bracing himself against the glove compartment.

They all turned and saw a large ram too close in front of them on the road, a sharp bend just ahead. The car swung violently as Roddy grabbed the wheel and lunged for the pedals, trying to regain control, but it was too late. They felt a huge jolt as they smashed into the ram, the car pitching sickeningly out of balance, spinning and skidding then tipping up onto its side, all in a blur, each of them trying to brace themselves for the impact, then suddenly they were upside down and tumbling, crunches, rips and screams filling the air as the car crumpled down the cliff side, Adam briefly noticing the thick, grey wall of cloud rolling in from the sea before he felt a sharp crack to his head, a white flash of incredible, burning pain, then everything went red then violet then black.

17

Soft, wet snowflakes landed on his face. How could it be
snowing in the car?

He opened his eyes and felt a jabbing pain at the back
of his head. He rubbed it with his hand, which came away
sticky with a trickle of blood.

The sky above him was thick, grey and heavy with snow.
Fat flakes fluttered casually down towards him, and he
blinked as one landed on his eyelash.

He pushed himself up on his elbows. He was lying in
spongy brown heather, and could smell the peat buried a few
feet below. His body ached, a jarring stiffness greeting every
muscle twitch. He gingerly moved each limb then rolled his
neck, his actions only met with grumbles, nothing sharper.

He looked round. Behind him was a sheer rocky cliff,
occasional mossy tufts poking out from pockets of scree.
It was at least 150 feet high. In the other direction, the sea
was shushing against the shore 100 feet below him, down an
incline peppered with boulders and craggy outcrops.

He sat up further and saw he was on a shelf in the cliff,
thirty feet of flat gorse and heather. He stood up. No sign
of the others. He walked to the edge of the shelf and saw
the Audi down below, mangled and upside down at a sharp
angle, almost at the water's edge. The front end was crumpled
into nothing, the left-hand side of the frame missing to reveal

the skeletal chassis underneath. He couldn't see from here if anyone was still inside.

He looked at his watch. The face was smashed and the display blank. He pressed the button for the heart-rate monitor. Nothing. Serenity now.

He pulled out his mobile and pressed 999. No bars on the signal, but worth trying. He heard a beep and looked at the screen – 'No network coverage'.

He checked the back of his head again. No new blood. He carefully edged his way down the slope towards the car. It was easier going than it looked from above, plenty of footholds and grips on the slanting rock face.

'Molly? Guys?'

He waited, listening. No reply, just the wash of the sea, his own heavy breathing and the thud of his heart in his ears. He bustled down the slope, breaking into a jog as the gradient eased off, a shuddering pain through his body with every step.

The car sat on a tiny rocky beach. He reached the passenger side first but there was no one there. He leant in and saw Molly and Roddy across the other side, hanging upside down in their seat belts.

'Molly, Roddy!' he shouted. No answer. 'Shit.'

He ran round to their side of the car and pulled on Molly's door, but it was buckled in the frame and wouldn't budge. He was standing in a rocky puddle of seawater, rainbowed with leaked petrol. He tried Roddy's door but it was the same. He shouted again, no answer.

He ran back round the car, looking for Ethan or Luke on the way. No sign. He climbed in the passenger side at the back and slid over to Molly. Her hair was tangled over her face. He reached out, swept it back and stroked her cheek.

'Molly? You OK? Please be OK.'

She blinked and moaned. 'Shit.'

'Thank God,' he said. 'Just hang on.'

She opened her eyes and looked at him. 'What . . .'

'Shhh, don't worry about it. We had a crash. I'm going to get you out. Can you move your arms?'

She tentatively stretched them out in front of her. It was weird seeing her movements upside down.

'OK, you'll need to brace yourself against the roof of the car. You're upside down. I'm going to release your seatbelt, so be ready. I'll try to hold on to you. OK?'

Molly nodded. He put an arm around her waist and reached for the red button of the seatbelt release. He pushed it and the buckle whizzed out of his hand, snapping downwards. He felt the sudden weight of her in his arms as she tumbled into him, knocking him onto the ceiling of the car and landing on him in a heap. Together they struggled out the other side of the car, scrambling onto the slick pebbles and breathing heavily.

'Thanks,' said Molly.

'You OK?'

She nodded. 'I think so.'

'Just wait here.'

He looked around for Luke or Ethan again. Nothing. He ducked into the car.

'Roddy?'

No answer. He turned Roddy's head towards him. Out cold. He touched his neck for a pulse, felt throbbing under his fingertips. He braced himself, wrapped an arm round Roddy's body and popped the seatbelt. He was pushed down by the weight, pain jabbing through his legs as he fell and Roddy's body pinned him to the ceiling. After a moment he felt Roddy shifting and saw Molly pulling at his arm. He pushed from the waist and slowly the body shifted off him and out the car. On the way past he felt something slick against his head. When Roddy's legs were clear he touched his face. Blood. He scooted clumsily out of the car.

Molly stood over Roddy, his face pale and his right shoulder a mess of blood. Adam went closer and saw a three-inch strip of jagged metal poking out from the fleshy part above his armpit.

'Jesus.'

'I know,' said Molly.

'What do we do?'

'Pull it out?'

'You think?'

'I have no idea.'

Adam knelt down and examined it. He tried to lift Roddy's jacket to see underneath but the spike pinned his clothes to his shoulder. He held the rod and gave it a gentle pull, but it was stuck firm. He tried again and blood oozed around the wound but the thing didn't budge. He gave another pull.

'What the fuck,' said Roddy, flinching and opening his eyes. 'Jesus fucking Christ, what're you doing to me?'

'Sorry, I was . . .'

Roddy let out a yell. 'Shit, that hurts.' He looked down at his shoulder. 'Oh, fuck.'

'Yeah.'

Roddy gazed at the spike sticking out of his shoulder, then touched the blood around the wound. He looked at Adam.

'What happened?' he said through gritted teeth.

'We had a crash.' Adam looked up. 'Came down that cliff.'
Roddy and Molly followed his gaze.

'Jesus Christ,' said Molly.

'What about this?' said Roddy, pointing at his shoulder.

Adam looked inside the car. The front windscreen frame was buckled and torn, bits missing. 'I think it's a bit of the car frame.'

Roddy winced. 'Fucking bullshit Audis. I knew I should've brought the Beemer.' He sat up carefully. 'Fucking help me up, then.'

Adam leaned in on his left side and lifted him. 'Don't you think we should get that out of you?'

'Fuck that,' said Roddy. 'If the pain I just felt when you pulled it is anything to go by, it can stay in there for-fucking-ever.' He tried to stretch a little and doubled over with pain, holding his arm. 'Fuck me.'

Molly and Adam looked at Roddy then at each other. Roddy righted himself, breathing heavily. He walked over to the car and looked inside. He gave the chassis a kick then cringed with pain. He turned and looked around.

'What happened to the other two?' he said.

'Good question,' said Molly.

18

Molly and Roddy tried their phones. Nothing. Adam looked up at the snowclouds then out to sea. It was starting to get dark.

'What time is it?'

Roddy looked at him. 'Your pulse gizmo fucked?'

Adam nodded and Roddy smirked. 'How are you going to cope without knowing how stressed you are?'

Molly looked at her phone. 'Ten past four.'

'Shit, we were unconscious for over an hour,' said Adam, trying to ignore Roddy. 'Ethan and Luke could be in a bad way.'

'We should split up and look for them,' said Molly.

Roddy leaned on a rock, then slid down onto his arse. 'Think I need to rest for a bit.' He fingered his shoulder. 'Feeling a bit dodge.'

'Should one of us try to get help?' said Adam.

Molly shook her head. 'It's freezing, the snow could get worse and it'll be dark soon. We need to find Ethan and Luke before we do anything else. Adam, you go left and I'll head right. After a couple of hundred yards head up the slope then work your way back along. I'll meet you up on the ledge if we haven't found anything.'

'OK.'

'I'll hold the fort here,' said Roddy, trying to laugh through laboured breaths.

Adam and Molly headed off along the beach. It was rough terrain, boulders and rocks everywhere, slippery kelp draped over low-lying stones.

Adam scrambled over the rocks as best he could, slithering around puddles and pools. He shouted for Luke and Ethan and heard Molly and Roddy doing the same, then as he cleared a large shelf of stone he spotted something. It was a body face down in a rockpool twenty yards away. He recognised the Berghaus fleece.

'Ethan,' he yelled, clambering over. He turned round briefly. 'Molly, over here, I've found Ethan.' He waited to see Molly wave in acknowledgement and change direction, then he clambered over to the body.

Something was badly wrong. The left arm and head were at impossible angles to the torso, which was slumped in half a foot of water. Adam turned him over, then staggered back with the force of lifting him. He sat next to the pool and looked at Ethan's face, one half of which was bloody and collapsed, the skull crushed, exposed empty eye socket glaring back at him.

He vomited into the water. His body shook as he heard Molly shouting to him. He looked up at Ethan again and winced. He edged towards the body and held Ethan's wrist with his own shaking hand. Freezing cold and no pulse. Fucking hell. Fucking, fucking hell.

'Oh, Christ,' said Molly behind him.

Adam dropped the hand and scuttled backwards.

Roddy appeared behind Molly. 'Holy fuck,' he said, turning away.

Adam sat on the ground shaking his head. 'I can't believe this is happening.'

Roddy looked at the body. 'Poor bastard.'

'Poor bastard?' said Adam, standing up. 'Roddy, this is all your fault.'

'How do you figure that?'

'If you hadn't been driving like a total maniac we wouldn't have come over that cliff and Ethan wouldn't be lying there with half his face missing.'

'If you hadn't punched me in the fucking ear when I was driving . . .'

'So this is my fault?'

'Fucking right it is.'

'You never take responsibility, do you?'

'Not if it's not my fault.'

'Bastard!' Adam shouted, rushing towards Roddy and swinging for him.

Roddy stumbled backwards clutching his shoulder and fell to the ground as Adam threw punches at his head and body. Roddy covered his face with his good arm, ducking out the way of the fists as best he could.

'Adam,' cried Molly, pulling at him. 'Leave him.'

Roddy brought his knee up into Adam's groin, making him collapse, then slid out from underneath, pinning him with his knees and punching with his left hand. Molly was forced back by the struggle as they swore and raged at each other like boys in the playground.

'What the hell are you guys doing?'

The voice was quiet but it made them stop and turn.

Luke was standing on a rock above them. He made an

agile leap down as Roddy and Adam rolled apart, wheezing and coughing.

Luke was about to speak when he saw Ethan's body. He walked over and knelt down next to him. He touched Ethan's neck in a tender gesture then put a hand on his own brow. 'Jesus.'

He shook his head and walked back to where they were standing.

'What happened, man?'

'We came over that cliff,' said Molly. 'Adam came round first and got me and Roddy out of the car. You and Ethan must've been thrown clear. Where were you?'

Luke nodded behind her. 'Up the slope, thick heather.' He looked at Ethan. 'I was lucky, I guess.' He noticed Roddy's shoulder. 'What happened to you?'

'That's the last time I buy a fucking Audi,' said Roddy. 'Came apart like balsa wood.'

'Looks sore, man.'

'Correct, Einstein.' Roddy grimaced. 'Give the man a medical degree. So I guess we go get help now.'

'Fucking hell,' said Adam.

'What?'

'Ethan's lying there dead, for Christ's sake.'

'So what?' said Roddy. 'We're supposed to sit around and grieve? Nothing we do changes what's happened. But we have to start thinking about getting the fuck out of here and saving ourselves.'

'You heartless bastard.'

'Heartless doesn't come into it. He's dead, that's that.'

'Jesus, someone is going to have to tell Debs,' said Adam.

They all stood in silence looking at the body.

'We have to get rescued first,' said Luke eventually. 'Phones?'

'Nothing,' said Molly.

'So what do we do now?' said Roddy.

'We need to think logically,' said Molly. 'Option number one is to stay by the car and wait to get spotted.'

'What are the chances of that happening?' said Adam.

Molly shrugged. 'Not great. We're very remote, and I don't think you can see the bottom of the cliff from the road. We could light a fire, that might get some attention, but not if there's no one nearby to see it.'

'Fuck that,' said Roddy. 'We need to do something. I'm not sitting around on my arse waiting to freeze to death.'

Molly nodded. 'Fair enough.'

She looked up at the cliff face. It was completely un-climbable.

'Well, there's no chance of getting back up that way,' she said, and turned to look both ways along the coast. 'Looks like we'll have to start walking, but it's not going to be easy.'

'Why not?' said Roddy.

'It's freezing cold, almost dark and the tide is coming in. Judging by where the grass starts, the water could come up another thirty yards.'

They all looked along the coastline. The shelf in the cliff petered out in both directions after a few hundred yards. Lower down, the beach was peppered with huge boulders in one direction, and hidden by a jutting headland in the other.

'We need to do something,' said Luke.

'Let's just start walking,' said Roddy.

'Which way?' said Adam.

'Well,' said Molly. She pointed in the boulder-strewn dir-ection. 'That's east, so Port Ellen is that way, but it's quite a few miles away, and I've no idea what the coast is like between here and there. What we can see from here doesn't look too easy to get across.'

She turned towards the headland. 'That way is the American Monument, it's definitely closer. I know there's a farm near it, Upper Killeyan, and a clifftop path at the monument, but I don't know if there's a way up from the beach.'

'What about mobile reception?' said Luke. 'Which way's better for getting a signal?'

Molly shook her head. 'There's no reception anywhere on the Oa. Hardly anyone lives here, there's never been a need.'

Roddy turned to Adam and laughed. 'You were going to start up your own business in a place that doesn't even have mobile reception? Jesus Christ.'

Adam glared at him.

'Oh, fuck you,' said Roddy, getting his coke tin out and tooting a line.

'I don't think that'll help,' said Adam.

'Fuck off, I need it for the pain.' Roddy waved the box around. 'Anyone want a line?'

They all stared at him, incredulous.

'Suit yourselves.'

'So which way?' said Luke eventually.

Snowflakes disappeared as they hit the wet ground around them, but left a thin white layer on their shoulders.

Adam shrugged.

'I think west,' said Molly, turning. 'The terrain looks easier and we know there's a farmhouse not too far away.'

'West it is,' said Roddy, snorting another line and sniffing.

19

The light was almost gone and snow covered the ground by the time they reached the bottom of the headland. Adam looked back the way they'd come, thin threads of footprints trailing back to the crumpled car, now being lapped by waves. He could just make out Ethan's body. He and Luke had dragged him the short distance to the car so he would be easier to find, and placed him above high tide, so he was lying twenty feet further up, a snowy bump marked by a small cairn.

Adam looked at the dried blood on his hands and felt sick, Ethan's death a rock in his stomach. How the hell had it come to this? Why Ethan? He was always the cautious one, the safe guy, the one who took out insurance and made sensible career moves and never did anything out of place. Surely he would've been wearing a seat belt? If not, why the hell not? Either way, he was now laid out at the bottom of a cliff, snow soaking into his bones, and the whole thing was Adam's fault, despite what he'd yelled at Roddy earlier. This morning outside the B&B, Ethan had talked about going home to see Debs, but Adam had talked him out of it. Jesus Christ. He felt his stomach heave.

'Look.'

Molly was pointing ahead. Luke and Roddy were just behind him, and the three of them hurried to reach her.

In the far distance Adam could see a light. It was a couple

of miles away at least, and the night encroached all around, but there was definitely something there.

'Looks like a farmhouse,' said Molly.

Adam peered into the darkness. There was an outline of a building nestled tightly into a cove just before the next headland. He couldn't see any other buildings, or any road or path leading to the place, but then it was hard to make anything out in the creeping gloom.

As they watched, the light blinked out, leaving a thin outline behind.

'Maybe they've closed the curtains,' said Molly.

'It's a bit in the arse-end of nowhere, isn't it?' said Roddy.

'Lucky for us it is,' said Adam. He squinted and thought he saw a whisper of smoke drifting up from the black shape, but couldn't be sure.

'Come on,' said Roddy in a strained voice. 'Let's get the fuck over there.' He held his injured arm tight to his body. 'I'm dying here.'

'You're not actually dying,' said Adam pointedly, glancing behind them.

'I might if we don't get a fucking bend on.'

It was slow going, even with the thought of the building spurring them on. The terrain was uneven, large slabs of rock and loose shingle-strewn slopes making it hard to find a way across, forcing them to take a time-consuming, circuitous route. They found themselves looping in and out, scrabbling up and over, having to detour around freezing pools of seawater and crumbling stone arches to make any headway.

Coming away from the sea and up the shore they found a path of sorts, a break in the stones underfoot, and they quickened their pace a little. It was dark now, and they kept losing the path in the snow, stumbling over rocks and into potholes, getting frantic as their fingers and feet began to sting with the cold. Adam wondered about frostbite: how did you know if you had it? He could still feel his extremities, but his whole body was visited by occasional shivering spasms as the snow got heavier all around. He looked ahead but all he could see was the thick black cliff face vaguely silhouetted against a gunmetal sky.

As he looked, an electric light appeared then disappeared, throwing the shape of a farmhouse into the inky night for a brief moment. It was enough to get their bearings. They were close now, just a few hundred yards away, and they hurried on, Molly and Adam ahead, Luke helping Roddy behind.

The path flattened out and Adam could suddenly hear something over the sound of the sea, the insistent rhythmic chug of a generator. He and Molly were almost at the building now, and he could make out a sliver of light at the bottom of the door. As they approached Adam realised it was a barn rather than a farmhouse, with no windows but a big, wide wooden door on the side facing them. He caught a whiff of a familiar smell as they reached the door and pushed it open.

'Hello? Anyone here? We need help.'

Adam and Molly walked inside.

The room was taken up by two large stills of beaten-up, discoloured copper, linked by ramshackle pipes to a rusting still safe. In one corner of the barn sat a grubby mash tun and a large steel washback, in the other were dozens of hogsheads and butts of different sizes and colours of wood.

'Holy crap,' said Molly.

'Is this what I think it is?' said Roddy.

'Yeah,' said Adam, looking around. 'An illegal still.'

'What the fuck's going on here?'

The voice from behind made them all turn.

Standing in the doorway was Joe in his police uniform, an impassive look on his face and a shotgun cradled in his elbow. Behind him was cousin Grant, tapping a side-handled baton against his leg.

20

Molly was first to move, walking towards him, hands out in front of her.

'Joe, thank God,' she said. 'There's been an accident.'

'Accident?'

'We drove our car over a cliff a few miles up the coast.'

'And you walked all the way here?'

Molly nodded.

Joe turned slowly from Molly to the rest of them.

'What happened to you?' he said to Roddy, pointing at his shoulder.

Roddy's face was pale in the striplit room. 'Got a piece of shit car stuck in me.'

'That Audi I pulled you up in?'

'Yeah.'

'*Vorsprung durch technik*, eh?'

'Fucking tell me about it.'

Joe looked around. 'Wasn't there another one in your gang?'

They all looked down.

'Ethan,' said Adam. 'He died in the crash.'

'So there's a smashed-up Audi and your mate's body at the bottom of a cliff round the coast?'

'Yeah,' said Molly.

'Which way?'

Molly looked confused and flustered. 'East, but never

mind that just now, we need to get to Bowmore Hospital, Roddy's shoulder needs fixed, the rest of us are probably close to hypothermia.'

'I'm just trying to get things straight,' said Joe. 'What were you doing on the Oa anyway?'

'Looking at the old Stremnishmore distillery,' said Adam.

'What for?'

'I want to start it up again.'

Joe laughed. 'Did you hear that, Grant?'

Grant smiled to reveal a snaggle of browning teeth.

'He wants to start up an old distillery, and now here he is standing in the middle of an illegal bootlegging operation,' said Joe. 'A bit suspicious, isn't it?'

'Don't be ridiculous,' said Molly. 'We got here just before you did.'

Roddy spoke to Joe. 'What are *you* doing here, anyway?'

Joe looked at him, then at Grant.

'Are you here to shut this place down?' said Adam.

Joe laughed and Grant joined in, a sharp bark of a sound.

'Not exactly,' said Joe, stepping further inside with Grant and closing the door behind him.

He lifted the shotgun and pointed it at them.

'We run this operation.'

The thrum of distillery equipment filled the silence between them for a few moments.

'Oh fuck,' said Roddy.

Molly looked at the shotgun and laughed nervously. 'Come on, Joe, don't be ridiculous.'

Joe levelled the gun at her as Grant took a pistol from the back of his trousers and pointed it at the rest of them.

'Get over with them,' Joe said to her.

'This is stupid,' said Molly. 'What are you doing?'

Joe walked up to her. 'I'm giving you an order, and I expect you to fucking obey it.'

'Why? Because you're the police, or because you're my dickhead ex-husband?'

He jabbed the shotgun butt into her stomach, winding her. She doubled over. He backhanded her across the face as she struggled for breath. She fell to her knees gasping.

'Now get your saggy fucking arse over with the rest of them where I can keep an eye on you.'

Molly struggled to her feet holding her face and shuffled over. They were standing in front of the larger of the two stills. Adam could feel the heat coming from it and smell the raw spirit in the air. He was starting to feel his feet again in his frozen shoes. His heart was bursting in his chest. He instinctively went for his watch then remembered it was broken.

Grant stood a few feet away, pointing the pistol. He had an ugly smile on his face, his eyes shifting between the four of them.

This wasn't happening. This couldn't be happening. Serenity fucking now.

Molly had recovered and was glaring at Joe. 'Look . . .'

'Shut up,' said Joe. He walked over to a beaten-up wooden table and chairs in the corner and slumped in a seat. The table was covered in junk – oily bits of machinery, plastic and glass bottles, petrol canisters, sheets of paper and strips of cloth. Joe lifted one of the canisters, unscrewed the lid and took a swig. He put the lid back on.

'Heads up, Grantie.'

He flung the canister in Grant's direction. Grant fumbled as he tried to catch it with one hand while also keeping an eye on the captives. He picked the canister up, dusted it off and took a big hit. His eyes widened and he puffed out his cheeks, then he screwed the lid back on and dropped it.

'Joe . . .' said Molly.

Grant stepped close to Molly and punched her in the belly.

'He said shut up,' he said, edging backwards and raising the gun. 'How about you be a good girl and do what you're told?'

Molly was hunched over, struggling to get air in her lungs. She eventually straightened and looked at Grant. 'You're a moron, you know that?'

'That's an interesting point of view considering who's got the gun here,' said Grant.

'Haven't you ever wanted to get a life of your own?' said Molly. 'Instead of being Joe's pathetic lapdog?'

'Would you like me to punch your face next time?' said Grant.

'Shut the fuck up!' Joe screamed, jerking out of his seat and knocking the chair over. 'Jesus.'

He put his hand to the back of his head and walked around for a while, then turned to Grant.

'Watch them, I'll be back in a minute.'

Joe left the barn. Grant's eyes kept darting around, to the canister on the floor, over the four of them, at the spirit safe burbling away, never settling on anything. It made Adam queasy to watch.

After a couple of minutes Joe came back in carrying a jumble of plastic strips in his hand. He walked over and threw them on the ground at Grant's feet. Adam saw they were hand and foot restraints, the kind they used on terrorists, like giant cable ties.

'First things first,' Joe said to Grant. 'Tie these cunts up so they can't escape.'

He turned to look at the four of them, his eyes narrowing.

'Then we'll decide what the fuck to do with them.'

21

'This is ridiculous,' said Adam.

His arms were bent behind his back and he felt the restraints bite as Grant pulled them tight around his wrists. Grant tied his ankles and moved on to Molly, as Adam slumped down against a cask. 'You're breaking about a dozen laws.'

'We are the law,' said Grant quietly.

'You're not the only cops on the island,' said Molly. 'There are plenty of decent officers on Islay who would skin you alive for this shit if they found out.'

Joe smiled as he watched Grant work. 'Like who?'

'Eric Dalton for one.'

'Dalton?' Joe laughed. 'That old cunt couldn't find his arse if you handed it to him on a fucking plate, never mind uncover an operation like this. Anyway, he's virtually retired, it's pipe and slippers for him in a few weeks.'

'You'll never get away with this,' said Adam.

'Who's going to stop me? You?'

'What're you going to do, exactly? Kill us all?'

Joe mugged looking thoughtful for a moment. 'Kill you all, now there's an idea. I hadn't thought of that.'

Roddy screamed as Grant yanked his arms behind his back. 'Fucking cunt, that hurts.'

'Good,' said Grant.

Joe walked over and smiled as Grant secured Roddy's ankles.

'Aw, diddums,' he said. 'Did nasty little Grantie hurt the rich dickhead, did he?'

'Fucking right he did,' said Roddy, sweating. He didn't look well. His red eyes were watery and his face was washed-out grey. He seemed to be shaking, trying to control it. He gave Joe a thin smile.

'Fucking cocky cunt, aren't you?' said Joe.

'Takes one to know one.'

'I knew you were trouble when I first saw you driving that wankmobile.'

'Well, we're in agreement about that shit car, anyway.'

Adam tried to think back. Getting pulled over for speeding had been a day and a half ago, but it seemed like a lifetime. All he'd wanted was a couple of days on Islay, the chance to drink some malts and talk to Roddy about investing. How the fuck had they got into this shit?

Joe looked at Roddy. 'Your life's one big fucking joke, isn't it?'

'You've got to make the most of it.'

'You think you're better than everyone else, don't you?'

'I buy and sell people like you every day.'

'Is that right?'

'Fund manager.'

Joe snorted with laughter. 'Fuck, that's worse than paedophile at the moment.'

'Tell me about it.'

'You know what they do to paedos in prison, right?'

'Bake them a cake?'

Joe reached out and stroked the metal sticking out of Roddy's shoulder. He tightened his grip, twisted and pushed. Roddy let out an animal howl, writhing to escape then falling to his knees and struggling for breath. Blood seeped from the wound as Joe turned away.

'Not so fucking cocky now, are you?'

He went to the table and brought two chairs over for him and Grant. He picked up the petrol canister, took a swig and grimaced.

Grant finished tying up Luke then joined Joe. Luke sat next to the other three on the ground, leaning against hogsheads and facing the chairs.

'So,' said Joe. 'This is the part where you try to persuade me to let you go.'

'Please let us go,' Molly deadpanned.

Joe sat back and crossed his legs. 'You can do better than that.' He turned to Grant. 'Don't you think they can do better than that?'

'Maybe they don't want to live,' said Grant, smiling at Molly.

'Christ,' said Molly. 'You're a regular Morecambe and Wise, you pair.'

Joe ignored her and turned to Luke. 'What's the deal with you? Strong silent type?'

Luke gave a blank stare.

'Nothing?' said Joe. 'Not even to plead for your life?'

'You're not going to let us go,' Luke said.

Joe clapped sarcastically. 'Quite right. At least one of you cunts knows what's going on.'

'Look,' said Adam. 'You *can* let us go. We won't tell anyone about this place, I promise. Three of us will be off the island in hours anyway, and I'm sure Molly just wants to be left alone.'

Joe laughed hard. 'Didn't you learn anything from Quiet Boy over there? We're not letting you go. Then again, maybe I'm just saying that so you beg and plead and demean yourselves, then I'll let you go. Or maybe kill you. Life's complicated, isn't it, Grant?'

'These cunts have no idea how complicated it is,' said Grant.

'I'm confused,' said Roddy, recovering composure. 'Which one of you is the good cop? This is more of an "arse cop, twat cop" routine.'

Joe turned to Grant. 'He's funny, isn't he?'

'He thinks he is, but he's wrong.'

'Let's turn out their pockets, see what we've got.'

Grant went through their pockets, dumping everything in a pile on the floor. Mobiles, keys, wallets, money, the Viagras from Adam's pocket, a notebook of Luke's and Roddy's coke tin.

'What have we here?' said Grant, picking up the Viagras.

Joe turned to Adam. 'Problems getting it up, eh?'

'They're not mine.'

'And yet they were in your pocket. Guess how many times I've heard that down at the station?' He turned to Molly. 'You hooked up with Mr Floppy here yet? I never had any trouble in that department, eh, love?'

'Piss off.'

Joe picked up the coke case and opened it. 'Shit, there's enough in here to fuel the whole of celebrity London.'

'Personal use,' said Roddy.

'Like fuck, this is ten times what we need to do you for dealing Class As.'

'Double A, more like,' said Roddy. 'That's none of your usual Colombian crap cut to fuck, that shit is purest Bolivian medical-research grade.'

Joe tapped a line onto his hand and snorted.

'Hey,' said Roddy.

'Fuck me,' said Joe, eyes like saucers.

He passed the tin to Grant who copied him.

'Holy shit,' said Grant, wiping his nose.

Joe shook his head as if trying to dislodge something. 'I guess being a hedge fund cunt has its advantages.' He looked at Roddy. 'But I don't suppose it really prepares you for situations like this.'

'You really don't have to do all this,' said Adam. 'You're digging a hole for yourselves.'

Joe sauntered over and casually kneed Adam in the face, sending his head slamming into the cask behind him.

'Jesus wept,' said Adam.

'The only holes we'll be digging are the ones we need to hide your bodies.'

Molly shook her head. 'What happened to you, Joe?'

Joe stopped in his tracks and turned. 'What?'

Molly sighed. 'You weren't always like this or I wouldn't have married you, would I? Don't you remember what it was like in the beginning between us?'

Joe rolled his eyes. 'Spare me the amateur psychology lesson, darling.'

'Do you think your dad would've been proud of how you turned out?'

'Where do you think I learned how to become such a bastard?'

'You don't have to repeat his mistakes.'

'I don't *have* to, but it turns out it's fun.'

'What about your mum, then?'

'You leave Mum out of it.'

'How would she feel about all this?'

Joe walked towards Molly with a strange look on his face, then hesitated.

'I know things didn't work out with us,' said Molly. 'Our plans for a family and everything.'

Joe looked like he was about to interrupt, but didn't. He turned away and looked at a far wall.

'But you're better than all this, Joe,' she said softly. 'At least, the Joe I used to know was better than this. He would never have got mixed up in all this insane shit.'

Eventually Joe turned, giving a little sigh. 'Yeah, well, the Joe you used to know doesn't exist any more. Meet the new, improved Joe.'

'I don't think it's an improvement,' said Molly. 'Cutting yourself off from the world like this.'

'I'm not cutting myself off from anything.'

'You are. All this stupid evil bullshit is just an excuse so that you don't have to feel anything any more.'

'That's bollocks,' said Joe, glancing at Grant, who was pocketing the Viagras.

'I don't think it is,' said Molly.

'It's too late,' said Joe, walking up close to her and crouching down to stare into her face. 'It's far too late for all this shit.'

Their lips were almost touching now.

'It's never too late,' said Molly, her eyes staring deep into his. His eyes flickered between holding her stare and gazing at her lips, two inches from his own.

There was a burst of electrical static over the distillery machines. Joe held Molly's gaze for a few more seconds then sighed, stood up and turned. A tinny voice could just be heard coming from the junk on the table in the far corner. Joe walked over and picked up a police radio.

'Sounds like our pick-up's on its way,' he said to Grant. 'I'll deal with this outside, you keep an eye on the Fantastic Four, eh?'

He stopped on the way out, turned back and whispered something to Grant, who nodded.

Adam felt blood trickling from his nose into his mouth as he watched Grant point the pistol at them.

22

'You don't have to do this,' said Adam.

Grant came up to him, face to face. Adam could smell the bitter moonshine on his breath, see an alcoholic sheen on his forehead. His eyes were glassy slits, and Adam wondered how much he and Joe had been drinking. If they were rat-arsed it might be easier to escape; on the other hand it might make them more volatile.

'I know I don't have to do it,' said Grant, baring his teeth.

'I mean, Joe's clearly lost it, but you seem like a decent guy. You could help us get out, we'd back you up with the authorities. It's all Joe's doing, right?'

'You have no idea, do you?'

'What?'

'You think I don't love this shit?'

'Ah.'

'We're the law on this island, we rule the place, and we can do whatever the fuck we like. Including making a packet from bootlegging, and stopping anyone that gets in our way.'

Adam heard a laugh. It was Roddy. 'Nice going, Freud,' he said to Adam between wheezes. 'That really got to his inner good guy, didn't it?'

'At least I'm trying,' said Adam. 'What the hell are you doing, except bleeding everywhere?'

'That's kind of keeping me occupied at the moment.'

Joe came back in and chucked the radio on the table.

'Well?'

Grant smiled. 'You owe me a fiver.'

'Fuck,' said Joe, getting out his wallet. He handed the money over and turned to them. 'I bet Grantie that Hedge Cunt would try to persuade him to let you escape, he backed Mr Floppy to go for it.'

He patted Grant on the back. 'I'll get you next time, mate.'

'You two are unbelievable,' said Molly.

'Thanks,' said Grant.

'Who was on the radio?' said Adam.

Joe smiled at him. 'Why the fuck should I tell you?'

Adam shrugged then regretted it as pain shot through his wrists from the restraints. 'What does it matter if you're going to kill us?'

Joe cricked his neck casually. 'Nothing much to tell. We discovered the Ramsay brothers running this place a few months back and liberated it from them. Told them to keep their mouths shut if they wanted to stay alive. Molly, you know the Ramsay brothers, right? Pair of fucking retards. Anyway, me and Grant took over the place and since then we've been making shitloads of illegal whisky when we're not on duty, and often when we are. We sell it and make piles of money. Any questions?'

Molly chipped in. 'Other police are involved?'

'What makes you say that?'

'The police radio, stupid.'

Joe smiled. 'Of course, silly me. Yeah, we move shipments to the mainland every now and then, so we need a boat.'

'A police boat?' said Adam.

'Give the guy a Scooby snack.'

'So this is a big operation?'

'Now you're starting to realise why we can't let you go,' said Joe. 'It's not just about me and Grantie here. There are others with time and money invested in this whole business. Not that it matters, we still wouldn't let you go, even if it was only us.'

'This is all bullshit,' Roddy piped up.

'Beg your pardon?' Joe turned towards him.

'I said this is all bullshit. You're not going to kill us. You don't have the fucking bollocks.'

'Is that right?'

'It takes a real fucking maniac to do something like that, and you don't have it in you, either of you.'

Grant snarled at him. 'And you would know, having shot how many people, exactly?'

'I've handled a gun.'

Joe laughed. 'Clay pigeons on a stag do, aye? Let me tell you, I've shot people, and it isn't the psychological trauma cop dramas make it out to be, trust me.'

'Bullshit.'

Joe smiled at Roddy then took a handgun from the waistband of his trousers. He sauntered up to Roddy, then past him. In one fluid movement he lifted the gun to Luke's forehead and pulled the trigger. The crack made them all jump, as Luke's head smacked against the cask. Blood spurted from the hole at the front of his head as he slumped over and hit the floor with a soft thud.

'Luke!' shouted Adam. 'Fuck!'

'Oh my God,' said Molly under her breath.

'See?' said Joe, turning to them. 'Now maybe you smart-mouthed bastards will start taking this situation a bit more seriously, eh?'

He turned back to Luke and nudged the body with his toe. He leaned in closer to Luke's head and frowned, then stared at the cask Luke had been leaning against. He knelt down next to the body and grabbed Luke's hair, lifting his head out of a small sticky pool of blood and looking at the back of it. He frowned again, then turned.

'What the fuck?' he said to Grant. 'There's no exit wound.'

He stared at the gun in his hand as Grant walked over.

Grant examined Luke's head then sucked his teeth. 'Right enough.'

Joe dropped Luke's head, which landed with a thump, spraying up blood from the pool on the floor. He turned to the rest of them.

'Was your mate a fucking cyborg or something?'

Adam couldn't speak, felt bile rise in his throat. He looked from the body to Molly and Roddy, both their faces full of shock. Eventually Roddy spoke.

'What do you mean?' he stuttered.

'Point-blank range, execution style,' said Grant. 'You always get an exit wound.'

Joe frowned at his gun. 'This baby usually makes quite a mess on the way out as well.'

'You're a sick fuck,' said Roddy, face ashen.

'That's as may be, but it doesn't explain why the bullet didn't come out your mate's head.'

Adam swallowed hard then heard his own voice, weak and wavering. 'Metal plate.'

'What?' Grant turned to him.

Adam gulped in air. 'He's got a metal plate in his head.'

Joe raised his eyebrows. 'Really? Why?'

'Snowmobile accident,' said Roddy quietly.

'Well, I'll be fucked,' said Grant, shaking his head. 'How about that?'

Joe stood thinking for a moment. 'That's a bit of a cunt, really. Now I'm going to have to get that bullet out of there. Can't be too careful about incriminating evidence, you know.'

He wandered over to the table and examined the mess, then picked up a large claw hammer, felt the heft of it in his grip.

'No, wait,' said Adam, feeling his stomach lurch. 'Whatever you're thinking of doing, please don't.'

Joe came back over, gripping the hammer.

'I don't have any choice.'

He positioned himself next to Luke's head and grabbed the front of his jacket for leverage.

'I can't go around shooting people and leaving bullets in their heads, can I?'

He flipped the hammer round so that the claw end pointed forward.

'Don't,' pleaded Adam.

Joe took a deep breath and raised the hammer, then swung it down hard into the side of Luke's skull.

23

Adam screwed his eyes tight, but the awful sounds kept coming to him. He'd known Luke the longest of all, met him at the union in Freshers' Week first year; four hours later they were steaming drunk best friends. Now Luke was lying in a spreading pool of his own blood, his head being caved in by a fucking lunatic.

Adam opened his eyes and glanced at the mess of Luke's head, the blood and brains, skull and hair. He felt a rush of fury swell up inside him. His stomach spasmed and he vomited acrid liquid down his front. He spat and tried to wipe his mouth on his shoulder.

Joe turned, wiping blood and sweat away from his forehead and breathing heavily.

'Looks like we've got a squeamish one,' he said, taking a swig of peatreek from the canister.

'You're not going to get away with this,' said Adam.

'You going to stop me?' Joe let out a melodramatic laugh. 'I don't think so.' He shook his head as he got his breath back. 'It wasn't my fault, I only did it to prove a point. Hedge Cunt here said I didn't have the bollocks to kill someone, so I had to show him. If anything, it's his fault your bumchum is dead.'

'Fuck you,' said Roddy.

Joe tapped out a line of coke and snorted, then threw the

case to Grant who did likewise.

Molly stared at Joe. 'I knew you had turned into an evil bastard, but I never thought you were capable of this.'

'Just shows you, doesn't it?' Joe smiled. 'You're married to someone for years, you think you know them, but they turn out to have hidden depths.'

'You need help,' said Molly. 'Psychiatric help.'

Joe laughed. 'Fuck that, I'm not mad, just bad. And certainly dangerous to know. You of all people should appreciate that.'

'I don't know how you ended up this way, Joe, but it has nothing to do with me. Or the miscarriages, if that's what you're blaming.'

Joe strode towards her. He grabbed her jaw and turned her face towards him.

'I never said any of this was to do with you, did I?' he hissed. 'Why don't you just shut up with the psychoanalysing bullshit for once, eh?'

'I'm just trying to understand,' said Molly.

'Well don't.' He was still holding her face by the chin. He smiled and moved closer till he was inches from her. 'Remember all the fun times we had in that marital bed?'

'Joe . . .'

He turned to Adam. 'Did she tell you she likes a bit of rough stuff?'

'Jesus Christ,' said Adam.

'The odd slap or punch gets the juices flowing,' Joe said, turning to Molly. 'Doesn't it, dear?'

Molly looked him in the eye. Adam tried to imagine what the hell it had been like between them. Joe must've been a completely different person, that's all he could think. He looked at Luke's body and wanted to stick a gun in Joe's face, watch him suffer the way he'd made them all suffer.

'In fact, just talking about it is getting me horny,' said Joe.

Molly's eyes widened.

'Joe,' she said, shaking her head. 'Don't.'

He grabbed her and dragged her to her feet.

'Leave her alone!' Adam shouted as Molly struggled to break free. Joe had a tight hold as he kicked over the whisky cask she'd been leaning on and forced her to lie across it face down.

'Get those scissors, will you?' he said to Grant, who fetched them from the table.

Molly was struggling, so Joe smashed her head off the barrel to subdue her.

'Fucking leave her,' said Adam. He got up, then stopped as Grant pointed the shotgun at him. Grant handed over the scissors then stepped backwards, keeping the gun trained on Adam and Roddy.

Joe reached down and cut the restraints from Molly's ankles.

'Got to get those legs spread, haven't we?' he said with a grim laugh.

He pulled her jeans down and Molly screamed.

Adam looked away. The noise in the barn got louder, a crescendo of machine buzz flooding his ears. He focused on the growing sound, which slowly changed and grew to a deafening hiss and shriek. Suddenly he felt himself knocked backwards as a blinding flash of incendiary light exploded in his peripheral vision.

He looked up to see Grant waving his arms around cartoonishly, his body engulfed in flames. The side of the nearest still had exploded down its riveted join, a ragged hole in the copper spewing clear liquid and blue flame everywhere.

'Jesus fuck,' said Joe. He was on the ground next to Molly, where they'd been knocked over by the blast. He scrambled towards Grant and the still, but was pushed back by the heat. He ran to the table, picked up a fire extinguisher and pointed it at the inferno.

Adam felt something hit his foot. It was the scissors. He looked up and saw Molly slumped on the floor, jeans round her ankles, looking at him, then the scissors. He shuffled round, picked them up with his tied hands, knelt with his feet behind him and clumsily cut his ankle ties. He looked at Joe, who had his back to them, pointing the extinguisher at the still, then at Grant, who was rolling frantically around on the ground.

Adam ran over to Molly with the scissors in his hands still tied behind him, turned his back to her then spoke over his shoulder.

'Put your wrist ties in the scissors. Careful, I can't see what I'm doing.'

'OK,' she said, then after a moment: 'Cut.'

He forced the scissor arms together and felt something give under the pressure. She took the scissors from his hands and cut his ties. They both looked at Joe, who was still blasting the extinguisher at Grant. The noise and heat from the fire were ferocious. Molly pulled her jeans up and ran over to Roddy, who was watching them with wide eyes. She cut his ties and helped him up.

Adam kept an eye on Joe. The shotgun was on the ground next to Grant, both of them still aflame. Grant had stopped rolling. Adam could see the handgun in Joe's trousers. He felt a tap on his shoulder, and turned to see Molly indicating the barn door. Behind her Roddy was reaching for the coke tin discarded on the floor. They both ran past him towards the door. He turned to look at Luke's corpse then followed them, stopping briefly at the table to pick up a torch.

'Hey!'

Adam turned to see Joe coming towards them, dropping the fire extinguisher and pulling the gun from his waist-band.

'I don't fucking think so.'

Molly and Roddy were at the door and heading into the night as Adam bolted after them. He heard a sharp crack and felt a bullet whiz past his head.

He got to the door, ran outside and slammed it behind him. There was a latch on the outside, which he threw over. The door shuddered as Joe crashed into it, but held.

'I'll fucking kill you,' said Joe through the door, followed by two explosions as bullets ripped through the wood and fizzed into the snow.

Joe began to kick the door from the inside as Adam turned. Molly and Roddy were heading round the side of the barn and he ran to catch up. Around the other side they found a police car, but it was locked.

'What do we do now?' said Adam, breathless.

They heard a crash from the other side of the barn.

'Run,' said Molly.

Joe appeared round the corner and spotted them. They ran behind the car and found a narrow lane leading uphill. Shots rang out and they all ducked.

There was the sound of another explosion from inside the barn.

Joe looked in their direction, then back at the barn. 'Fuck!' he shouted, then ran inside, leaving the three of them hurtling up the lane into the freezing, snowy blackness.

24

They ran for a few hundred yards, stumbling in the darkness, Roddy supported between the other two. Adam's lungs burned, his chest heaved and his legs ached. At the brow of a hill he looked back and could just make out the silhouette of the barn below. It wasn't in flames. Maybe Joe had the fire under control.

'We need to work out a plan,' said Molly.

'What plan?' said Roddy, gasping. 'We just keep fucking running.'

Molly shook her head. 'We need to think.'

'Maybe he's busy with the fire,' said Adam. 'Maybe he won't come after us.'

Even as the words came out of his mouth, Adam knew they were bullshit.

'He'll come after us,' said Molly. 'He can't let us live now, even if he wanted to before, which he didn't.'

'This is a total clusterfuck situation,' said Roddy.

'Quite,' said Molly.

'I can't believe he killed Luke,' said Adam, shaking his head and staring at his feet.

'I know,' said Molly. 'But we can't think about that now, we have to concentrate on getting out of this in one piece.'

'What do you suggest?' said Adam.

Molly looked back at the barn, getting her breath back. 'Once he gets the fire sorted he'll come after us. He'll have guns and he'll use the car. Which means we have to get off this path, it's too exposed. He can find us too easily.'

Adam turned the torch on and swept it around them. There was just snowy heath and moorland in every direction.

'And we can't use the torch,' said Molly, 'except in emergencies. It'll only flag up our position.'

Adam switched the torch off.

'It would be good if we could find some trees,' said Molly, scuffing her feet in the snow. 'We're leaving tracks.'

'We're fucking dead,' said Roddy.

'Don't say that,' said Adam.

'We are,' said Roddy. 'We can't move fast, we're in the middle of fucking nowhere, we're leaving tracks in the snow, it's pitch black and freezing, I'm bleeding to fuck, and we have no idea which way to go to get help.'

'Not entirely true,' said Molly. 'Remember, I said there was a farmhouse near the American Monument, at Upper Killeyan? I'm pretty sure it's that way.'

She waved off to the left in an unconvincing gesture.

'If we make it there, we can get help. If there's no one in the place, we can use the phone.'

'Shit,' said Adam. 'We should've taken the police radio from the table, shouldn't we? Used that to get help.'

Molly shook her head. 'We can't use a police radio, we've no idea who's listening in, whether they're on Joe and Grant's side or not. Joe used the radio to contact his pick-up guys, remember?'

'So if there's no one at this farmhouse and the phone works, who do we call?' said Roddy.

'Ash.'

'Ash?' Roddy sounded incredulous. 'She's our big escape hope?'

'Screw you,' said Molly. 'She's my sister, and if I call asking for help, she'll come get us.'

'What about that cop you mentioned to Joe?' said Adam.

'Eric?' Molly thought for a moment. 'I know he won't be messed up in any of this, but he's only one old guy, I don't know how much he can do. He could maybe come get us, but I wouldn't want him taking on Joe.'

'Is there any chance of a mobile reception anywhere out here?' said Adam. 'Should we have got our phones from the barn?'

'No point,' said Molly. 'We're further from Port Ellen than we were at the crash site, so if we couldn't get anything there, there's no chance out here.'

She looked into the darkness in the direction of the American Monument.

'The only problem with getting to this farmhouse is that there are loads of sea cliffs over that way as well.'

'Fucking great,' said Roddy.

'But if we're careful, we'll avoid them.'

'In the dark without the torch? Great plan.'

Molly stared at him in the gloom. 'You got a better one?'

Roddy glared at her for a long time then lowered his head. 'No.'

'Right. How are we all doing?'

Adam nodded. 'Good to go, I think.'

Roddy sighed. 'Fucked, but no more than when I woke up with half a fucking Audi in my shoulder.'

'You can move OK, yeah?' said Molly.

Roddy snorted sarcastically. 'Think so.'

Adam looked at Molly. 'And how are you?'

'Fine.'

'I mean, after . . . you know. Back there.'

'I said I'm fine.'

'What a fucking cunt,' said Roddy.

'Yeah, well,' said Molly.

They heard a noise and looked down the path. The snow was falling thicker now, but they could see a spread of light splaying out from the barn as the door opened. There was the metallic click and clunk of a car door opening and closing, followed by a pair of headlights suddenly blazing, beaming across the moor. The engine revved.

'Time to move,' said Molly. 'Any questions before we get going?'

'Yeah,' said Roddy, 'how the fuck did we get into this mess?'

25

They staggered frantically across the peat moors as best they could in the darkness, torn between watching where their feet were going and looking nervously behind them. After a couple of minutes they saw the sweep of the police car's headlights emerge over the hill, fingers of light reaching across the landscape. They flattened themselves into a small snowy crevice in the heather, freezing and soaking their stomachs, Roddy stifling a cry of pain.

The car crawled along the path, the beam of a torch coming from the driver's seat, spraying this way and that as Joe hunted for them. The car seemed to take forever to drive on, but eventually it crawled further along the path, heading inland, the headlights and torch beam arcing further away.

'Come on,' said Molly, picking herself up and trying to brush the wet snow off. 'This way.' She pointed uphill.

'Why that way?' said Roddy.

She helped him to his feet. 'Because it's the opposite direction from Joe. Good enough?'

'That'll do for me.'

They walked on, almost getting used to the rough terrain, the spongy feel of the heather under their feet, the snow smothering everything, the faint whiff of peat crystallising in the frozen air. The snow seemed to muffle all noise except for the squeak and scrunch of their footfalls in the white wilderness.

'Think he's lost us,' said Adam eventually, looking back. It had been quite a few minutes since they'd seen the lights from Joe's car.

'Fucking idiot,' said Roddy, as faint headlights appeared again on the horizon. 'Don't you know anything about tempting fate?'

'Remind me to kill you when we get out of here,' said Adam.

'Get down you morons,' hissed Molly, hitting the deck.

They did likewise as the car beams played over the hill they were on. They were more exposed than before, Adam suddenly regretting his dark jacket, an easy target against the white blanket covering everything.

The headlights passed over them. Adam looked up to see where the car was, just as the thinner beam from the torch pointed right in his face.

'Stay down,' said Molly, but it was too late.

The sound of a shot cracked the heavy silence, making them all jump.

'Shit,' said Molly.

She hauled Roddy up and started running, the three of them tumbling over rocks and holes, running for their lives. They darted from side to side, zigzagging as best they could.

The car headlights disappeared, but the beam of torch-light occasionally found them, causing them to scatter like panicked deer.

'Stay together,' shouted Molly over her shoulder. 'Or we're screwed.'

Adam grabbed Roddy and dragged him towards Molly, all of them trying to dodge the torchlight. His heart pounded in his ribcage and his head throbbed with the effort of trudging and slipping across the moors. This couldn't go on forever, something had to give one way or the other. He had a flicker of memory, sitting in front of a log fire in the Scotch Malt Whisky Society in Leith with the others, single-cask Laphroaigs in hand, Islay map laid out in front of them, getting psyched about the trip. It was a different universe.

The sound of a shot startled him, and he pulled Roddy on.

'Easy there, fuckface,' said Roddy.

'Shut up and run.'

'I'd run better if you stopped fucking pulling me.'

'Fine.' Adam let go. 'Suit yourself.'

He darted sideways and stumbled, lumbering forwards then pitching face first into the snow. He jumped back up and ran towards Roddy and Molly just ahead. Another shot rang out as the torch beam arced over them.

Joe couldn't be that close behind or he would've hit one of them by now. All Adam could hear was the rush of adrenalin and blood in his ears and his wheezing breath as he reached the top of a rise and dived over the other side. He began sliding downwards in the snow, caught a jumbled glimpse of Molly and Roddy doing the same a few yards ahead. He was picking up speed and so were they, all three of them out of control in the deepening snowdrifts. His feet sank deep into the white, pitching him over onto his stomach, then tumbling onto his back, out of control, sending a spray of snow up into his face as he keeled over, his momentum driving him down the slope, further and further, no idea which way was up and which was down, whether he was falling to safety or over a cliff edge. He panicked as he tried to regain his footing, felt a sharp smack as his arse hit a rock, throwing him over again, a weight of snow thrust down on top of him as he slid backwards for a few more yards before thumping into something soft.

'Fuck.'

It was Roddy beneath him, Molly a couple of yards to the side. Adam rolled over and looked back up the slope.

A blaze of burning light exploded into the air, making him flinch and close his eyes. He shook his head and opened them again. The snow all around was bathed in luminous violet light, giving everything an eerie, nightmarish look. Standing at the top of the hill was Joe holding a huge flare spewing out smoke and light. In his other hand was a gun. He was scanning the whiteout, looking in the other direction, so he hadn't yet spotted them half buried under a mini-avalanche.

'Fuck,' said Roddy as Joe turned towards them.

Adam looked beyond Roddy. In the distance he could see the American Monument, its lighthouse shape penetrating the purple edge of sky. Between here and there was an oddly flat expanse, the white sheen covered in thousands of small dark shapes.

'What the hell is that?' said Adam.

Joe's gaze finally rested on the three of them, far enough away that they were still a tricky shot from the top of the hill.

Molly got up and started running. 'Our salvation,' she said over her shoulder, as Adam and Roddy picked themselves up and pitched after her.

26

Adam only realised it was a frozen loch when he slipped and landed on his arse. They were running on ice. Roddy let out a derisive snort somewhere behind him.

'Come on, clumsy-arse,' Roddy said, jogging past him.

Adam looked back. Joe was tripping and sliding down the hill in a flurry of snow, the flare held high, casting a surreal indigo sheen over the land like some strange alien visitation.

Molly was up ahead, running at the thousands of dark shapes scattered across the middle of the ice. As she got closer, she began waving her arms frantically over her head, whooping and shrieking for all she was worth.

'What the hell is she doing?' said Adam.

'Fuck knows.'

They hurried forward, gaining on her, and just as they were getting close, the dark shapes began moving, rising up into the sky above, then suddenly they were all around them in a cacophony of hooting and hissing and flapping.

'Fucking geese!' shouted Roddy.

They covered their heads as they sprinted on, thousands of newly woken geese causing chaos in the air and on the ground. The birds were swooping and swerving, soaring and diving over and beyond them as they caught up with Molly and joined her in scaring more birds into the already crowded air.

Adam looked back and couldn't see Joe amongst all the

mayhem. If they couldn't see Joe, Joe couldn't see them, right? Under the cover of the geese's frenzied activity, Molly shouted to them.

'That way.' She pointed to their left. 'I'm pretty sure the farmhouse is just beyond that ridge.'

They started into a crouching run, occasionally ducking as a bird got close with its beak or wings, Adam glancing round to see where Joe was. The purple light was in the centre of the loch now, surrounded by thousands of squawking geese, angry at being woken up. They were making hysterical shapes in the sky, racing panic-stricken up and down, skidding on the ice and stumbling over each other. Adam ran faster, spurred on by the sight of Joe stuck in the chaos.

Near the edge of the loch, Adam felt the ice give way underneath him. An almighty creak, then the ice split in two, white sliced by spreading black, and Adam found himself running on nothing for an instant before slumping into freezing water, the chill of it shocking the breath out of his body as he scrambled and clawed at shifting chunks of ice for purchase.

Molly and Roddy had already disappeared into the darkness ahead. They hadn't seen him go through the ice. His head ducked under the surface. The cold of the water stung his face like pins. He thrashed his arms and legs and his head bobbed above the surface for a moment, but his lungs refused to work, and he sank back under, getting a mouthful of icy water as he went.

It felt like his heart was going to burst out of his chest, his ears full of raging noise as his arms and legs flailed again. His body shook with cold, he was losing feeling in his hands and feet. He made a supreme effort to get his head above water. Through the water streaming down his face he thought he saw a hand and made a lunge for it, missing as his body bobbed and pitched. He was sucked under again, panicking. He made a final, huge effort to push himself upwards, legs and arms aching. He scrabbled frantically for the hand. Just as he was sinking again, he felt his hand clutched by grasping fingers and held on for his life.

He felt the hand move, pulling him up and out of the water. As he scrambled forward he saw it was Molly holding him, grim determination on her face as she lay on the ice. Roddy lay behind her, holding her legs with his good arm.

Adam felt solid ice under his chest now and kicked his legs, squirming violently, flapping his way out of the water. He felt his waist snag on a jagged crust of ice and wriggled free, swinging a leg over onto more solid stuff. His other leg followed and he lay for a moment gasping and coughing, his body shaking violently from the cold, shock and adrenalin.

Molly shuffled backwards across the ice on hands and knees like a commando, dragging him as she went. He tried to get onto his feet.

'No, stay flat out,' she said. 'Spread your weight.'

He moved with her for thirty yards then they rose to their knees, then their feet, Roddy joining them. They were at the edge of the loch now, running through frozen reeds which whipped and cut them as they tumbled forwards.

Adam glanced behind. The light from the flare was fading, but in the violet gloom it looked as if the geese had settled again, only a few still flying, the rest back on the ice honking unhappily. As he watched there was another blinding flash of purple light – a new flare. Shit, Joe probably had a whole belt full of the fucking things. This was never going to end, was it?

'Do you think he knows which way we went?' Adam said, breathless and shivering.

'What, you mean apart from the tracks in the snow and the big fucking hole you left in the ice?' said Roddy.

27

'There.'

Molly pointed. The blanket of cloud overhead had broken into clumsy chunks of grey, moonlight coming and going, illuminating a dark geometric shape against the snowy curves of the land. The farmhouse. No lights on, but then it was the middle of the night. Adam looked at his broken watch without thinking, and saw that his hands were shaking. He tried to stop them.

'Is that your teeth chattering?' said Roddy.

Only now that he mentioned it did Adam realise it was. He felt convulsions jerking into life across his body.

Molly's face was pinched with concern. 'We need to get you out of those clothes.'

She looked back the way they'd come. No purple flare, no sign of Joe. Everything seemed deathly quiet after the madness of the geese on the ice. She turned to look at the farmhouse.

'Hopefully we'll be able to get dry clothes at the house.'

They reached the front gate in a few minutes, staggering up the path, banging on the door and shouting.

'Hello? Anyone there? We need help.'

There were no vehicles visible, no lights on, no signs of life.

Roddy kept banging on the door with his good hand as Molly went round the back. Adam watched the way they'd come for any sign of Joe, but was unable to concentrate, his body feeling like electric currents were being passed through it, jerking and locking, his muscles burning, his lungs suddenly shallow.

'Fucking hell,' said Roddy. 'There's no cunt here.'

They heard glass smash from the other side of the house.

'Molly?' said Adam, stuttering the word out.

They stood there listening, not knowing what to do. A minute later the door opened and Molly stood there shaking her head.

'Nobody home. Doesn't look like it's been occupied for the winter. The phone line's dead as well. Either they didn't pay the bill or the snow's taken the lines down.'

'Bollocks,' said Roddy.

Molly guided the shivering Adam through the door into the hall, Roddy following behind, shaking his head. Molly turned to him, pointing at Adam.

'Help him get his clothes off.'

'Really?'

'Yes.'

'All of them?'

'Yes.'

'Why?'

'He's going to die otherwise.'

She looked around, began opening doors, found a linen closet. She pulled out two large towels and handed them to Roddy.

'Then dry him off.'

'No fucking way.'

Molly rolled her eyes upwards. 'Just do it.'

'You do it, I'm not touching his naked body.'

'You're pathetic,' said Molly. 'You really are.'

'J-J-Just n-do it,' said Adam, fumbling at his sleeve with trembling fingers.

Molly was already down the corridor. 'I'll find some new clothes for him.'

Roddy sighed and approached Adam, moving his shaking fingers aside. 'Out the way, you handless fuck, let me do it.'

It was slow going with one good arm, peeling off the frozen clothes and dumping them on the ground. Roddy grimaced as he rubbed Adam's arms, legs and torso with one towel, Adam trying to dry himself with the other one. By the time they'd finished his shaking had eased off, just little tremors rippling through his jaw and chest. Adam wrapped both towels around him and stared at his pale, exposed legs.

'Looking good,' said Roddy, as Molly appeared with an armful of clothes.

'Shut up, Roddy,' said Molly as she started helping him on with jeans, socks, shoes, T-shirt, two jumpers and a fleece. Everything was a bit big for him, but not too bad. When they'd finished, Adam picked up the torch he'd placed on the ground and put it in the fleece pocket.

'You look ridiculous,' said Roddy.

'You're not helping,' said Molly. 'I'm trying to keep him alive and get us out of this shit.'

Roddy looked at her. 'So you should, it's your ex-husband who's trying to fucking kill us.'

Molly stared at him. 'You think I don't know that?'

'Didn't you have any inkling he was a psychopath when you said "I do"?'

'Shut up, Roddy,' said Adam.

Molly had her hands on her hips. 'So you're saying it's my fault Joe's after us?'

'Who else's fault is it?' said Roddy.

'That's bullshit,' said Adam. 'With or without Molly, he wouldn't have let us go once we'd seen the still operation.'

'We don't know that,' said Roddy.

Adam lunged at Roddy's injured shoulder.

'Ow, fucking hell,' said Roddy, buckling.

'Take it easy, Adam,' said Molly.

Adam turned to her. 'You've got nothing to feel bad about. Jesus, you've already saved our lives at least twice.'

Silence for a moment, a strip of silky moonlight stretching across the hall from the open doorway.

'You all right?' Molly said to Roddy.

Roddy glared at the pair of them and let out a laugh more like a gasp. 'You mean apart from the large wound and heavy blood loss?' He coughed a dirty, ragged cough. 'And this cunt attacking me? Fine, thanks.'

'Sorry,' said Adam. 'But you were out of order.'

'Fuck you.'

In the moonlight Adam could see Roddy was sweating heavily. He looked like a ghost.

'So what do we do now?' said Adam, his shivers receding further.

'Are you OK?' said Molly.

Adam nodded. 'Feeling a lot better now, thanks for that.'

Roddy snorted. 'When you're quite finished sticking your tongue up her ass, can someone please tell me what we're going to do now?'

'You're going to die.'

The voice from the doorway made them all jump.

Joe was silhouetted against the moonlight, pistol in hand. He was sweating and breathless, but smiling widely.

'Fuck,' said Roddy.

Joe laughed. 'Thought you had me with that goose thing, eh? Hey, I just realised, that was literally a wild goose chase, wasn't it?'

They stood motionless. Adam had his hands in his fleece pockets, his fingers gripping the handle of the torch. Joe was still getting his breath back, so Adam took a chance. He jerked the torch out of his pocket, switching it on in the process, and hurled it at Joe's head, the beam of light slicing through the air as it span. Joe ducked instinctively as the torch came towards him, giving them a moment of distraction.

'Move!' Adam shouted, pushing Roddy and Molly down the corridor and heading after them, Molly leading them frantically through to the kitchen then towards the back door.

Joe roared after them. Adam ducked as a bullet ripped past his head. He reached for a chair and hurled it behind him, saw it smash off Joe's body as he came through the kitchen doorway, knocking him with a hard thump into a heavy stone worktop then onto the ground.

Adam was out the back door and sprinting across a field of sleeping sheep, Molly and Roddy stumbling and tripping ahead. They ran and ran, losing their footing but blundering on regardless, the sheep around them fluttering in a vague panic. They climbed over fences and ran through snowdrifts until the farmhouse was out of sight. Adam realised he was shaking with the effort as they slowed to a nervous walk.

The snowclouds above had vanished, the whole land bathed in moonlight. They kept walking. Adam glanced back, but saw only sheep. Joe must be coming after them, but where was he? He wouldn't give up now, no way.

The field they were in was adjacent to a clifftop, and the moonlit sea far below was rippling quicksilver. They reached a large rock and stopped to get their breath back.

'We can't go on like this,' said Roddy, gasping and shaking.

'I know what you mean,' said Adam, unable to control his convulsing body. He felt like he might pass out any second. He leaned against the rock as if it was the softest bed in the world.

Molly nodded.

'We need to confront him,' she said. 'Set a trap.'

'Shit,' said Adam, feeling dizzy. 'Really?'

Roddy spat and snorted. 'She's right. We need to end this.'

Adam looked at the two of them. 'Anyone got any ideas?'

Molly nodded. 'I think so.' She pushed herself up from the rock. 'Come on, follow me.'

'I'm scared to ask,' said Adam. 'But where?'

'Back to the still. There's stuff there we can use, maybe. Either way, it ends there.'

Molly started walking. Adam looked at Roddy, who just shrugged.

'Right,' said Adam, as he and Roddy scurried after her in the powdery snow.

28

They stood at the edge of a high cliff on the protruding headland and looked down. They could see the still below, the watery moonlight giving it a sharp, spectral appearance. Adam noticed a thin wisp of smoke or steam coming from the building and wondered how much fire damage there was.

They'd walked as fast as possible across the snow-crumpled fields and moors of the headlands, a jittery spring in their steps at the thought of what was to come. There was no sign of Joe following behind. Adam didn't know how this would pan out, but they couldn't keep running forever, and besides, they had nowhere else to go.

A gunshot cracked the silence. Hitting the ground fast, they shuffled to look behind to where the noise came from.

Far away in the distance a torch beam was flashing on and off.

They lay in silence for a moment.

'The cunt's playing with us,' said Roddy. 'Like he's stalking prey. Just letting us know he's still on our trail.'

He was too far away to have realistically taken a shot at them; it was a warning.

'What a prick,' said Adam.

'Took the words right out of my mouth,' said Molly, getting up and turning. 'Come on, let's get down there and get ready. As ready as we can be, anyway.'

There was a steep path cut into a cleft in the cliff, and they carefully edged their way down it in the ice and snow, wary that one slip could send them tumbling hundreds of feet onto rocks.

Roddy grunted and groaned as they went, stopping often to rest and snort coke, much to the other two's disgust. They were all sweating from the exertion. Adam was thankful for his umpteen layers of dry clothes, but the freezing air still bit at him, his hands and feet numb. He wondered again what frostbite felt like. He'd seen Arctic explorers on television with blackened stumps at the ends of their wrists and ankles. Jesus wept.

They reached the bottom and scuttled across flat terrain to the barn in a whiteout silence.

Molly carefully pushed the door open. The electric light inside was momentarily blinding after so long in thin moon-light.

As his eyes got accustomed, Adam saw the same scene of carnage they'd left a while ago. One of the stills ripped open, charred metal and wood around it, gallons of spirit pooled on the floor alongside. Grant's body was burnt-out black, lying in a spread of fire-extinguisher foam. The barbecue smell of cooked meat made Adam gag as he reached to cover his nose and mouth. Across the room, Luke was slumped sideways against the hogshead cask in a circle of dark red.

Adam went over to him and knelt down. One side of his head was caved in, thanks to Joe and the clawhammer, the eye socket raw and bloody, but the rest of his face had the same implacable look he had when he was alive. Adam reached out and touched his cheek, then recoiled at the rubbery feel of the flesh, already cooling, thickening and hardening. It was unbearable. First Ethan, now Luke, it was all so fucking horrific. If he hadn't dragged them on this ridiculous trip, they'd all be safe back in the Leith tasting rooms now, winding each other up and necking a rare Caol Ila or a fresh new Ardbeg first-fill cask.

The thought of whisky made him turn. The petrol canister that Joe and Grant had been drinking from was on the floor. He opened it and took a sniff. Raw, obviously, but he wiped the rim and took a sip, sloshing it around his mouth. Fuck. They weren't just making gut-rot here, this stuff was actually drinkable, notes of salty sea breeze and pine nuts amongst coal smoke rather than peat. He'd tasted worse, put it that way. A lot worse.

'What the fuck are you doing?' said Roddy. 'Are you tasting those cunts' moonshine?'

Adam looked guilty as Roddy grabbed the canister and took a big glug.

'Shit, that's halfway decent.'

'I know.'

'When you boys are quite finished,' said Molly, at the table now, 'maybe you could help me look for something useful.'

'Like what?'

'How the hell should I know? Something that'll help us get out of this nightmare. Use your imaginations. I've never been hunted down by a maniac before, strangely enough.'

Roddy took another big drink then winced. The colour drained from his face. His shoulder had to be hurting.

Molly raked over the junk on the table. 'This is all just crap,' she said. 'Nothing much we can use here.'

Roddy was resting against the back of a chair, trying to get his energy back, canister in hand.

'Shouldn't we have a lookout at the door?' said Adam.

Roddy shook his head. 'You saw how far behind he was, we've got ages yet.'

'Just go over and watch out for him, Roddy, eh?'

'You fucking do it, if it's such a great idea.'

Adam sighed. He searched round the back of the still and found something.

'Look.'

He brought out a large, beaten-up toolbox and dumped it on the table. The metal handles were sore against his fingers, but that meant the feeling was coming back into his hands. The heat in here was thawing him again.

He opened the toolbox. It was rammed with all sorts of stuff, wrenches and spanners, a crowbar, screwdrivers and hammers. They started sizing up weapons in their hands as Adam lifted the top section out. Underneath were a handheld power drill and a blowtorch.

'Now we're talking,' said Roddy, lifting the drill out. He pointed it at Adam, pulled the trigger and the room filled with a high-pitched whiny whir.

'Cut it out,' said Adam, taking out the blowtorch. He turned it in his hands, getting a feel for it. It was quite flashy, like a modern hairdryer or something. He found the gas valve and turned it, then clicked the ignition and a jet of blue flame shot out the nozzle towards Roddy.

'Easy, Tiger,' said Roddy, backing away.

Molly took two aerosols out of the bottom of the toolbox and displayed them – one pesticide, one anti-freeze.

'What do you reckon these are for?'

Adam looked at the moonshine canister and sucked on the chemical aftertaste in his mouth. 'Hmmm.'

She chucked them back into the box and surveyed what they had.

'This is all good, but we don't have anything to match a gun.'

Adam switched the blowtorch off. Roddy whirred the power drill in the air.

'We'll just have to use the element of surprise.'

'How exactly do we do that?' said Adam. 'He knows we're here.'

'I have no idea,' said Roddy. 'It's just the kind of thing people say in situations like this.'

Molly sighed.

'Well, he'll be here soon enough, so we'd better think of something quick.'

'Too late,' said Joe, grinning at the barn door and pointing a gun at them.

Their faces crumpled.

'I told you we should've had a bloody lookout,' Adam said to Roddy.

'Fuck you,' said Roddy.

'You should've listened to your bumchum,' said Joe. 'He was right for once.'

29

'How the fuck did you get here so quick?' said Roddy.

Joe pulled car keys out of his pocket and dangled them.

'After sending you that wee signal with the torch, I cut inland back to the road. I knew you'd think I'd follow you across the cliffs. I also knew you'd come back here. Actually, I hoped I might get here first, but no matter.'

Adam looked at Joe. His cheeks were red and there was a watery sparkle in his eyes. He looked like he was having the best time of his life.

'Don't kill us,' pleaded Adam.

'Succinct and no-nonsense,' said Joe. 'But completely pointless. Of course I'm going to kill you, why do you think I've just fucking chased you halfway around the Oa in the snow at night? To give you a pat on the back? Dickhead.'

Radio static jumped out at them.

Joe kept his eye and gun on them as he reached for the radio on his belt.

'Yeah?' he said into it.

The voice on the other end spoke, but they couldn't make out what was said.

'Half an hour's cool,' said Joe, winking at them. 'I'll have everything ready for you then.'

He put the radio back in his belt.

'How are you going to explain all this to your mates on

the radio?' said Molly, waving an arm around the scene behind them.

Joe put a finger to the corner of his mouth. 'They never need to know about you three fuckwits, or laughing boy over there.' He waved the gun at Luke's body.

He turned to look at Grant. 'And let me tell you, no one is going to miss that arsehole, least of all the people I work with. Grantie was a liability, and we all knew it. As for the still, well that can always be fixed. There's enough money being coined in here to make it worth our while.'

'But how are you going to explain away our deaths?' said Adam.

Joe sighed. 'You really have no fucking clue, do you? I won't have to explain anything, there won't be any bodies. I'll get rid of the evidence in the still furnace over there. No bodies, no crime. You cunts came to the island, then you left and took Molly with you.'

'People will come looking for us,' said Roddy.

'You think so?' said Joe. 'You've got a pretty high opinion of your own importance. Even if someone does come, I just put on the friendly policeman face, say I'll look into it, and everyone buggers off thinking I've got it in hand.'

Molly gave it one last go. 'No one from the island is going to believe I just upped and left with four guys from the mainland, without a word to anyone.'

'Then you'll just have to be a missing person.' Joe shrugged. 'What else can I do?'

'You don't have to do anything,' said Molly. 'Let us go. Don't make it any worse than it already is. There's still a way out of this for all of us.'

Joe snorted a sickly, desperate laugh. 'Look around you, darling.' He waved his gun around the room. 'Does it look like there's a way out for me now? Does it?'

'You have to stop all this,' said Molly calmly.

Joe shook his head and lowered his voice. 'I can't stop, Molly. That's just it. Can't you see? I can't stop. This is what I do now. This is who I am.'

He looked at her for a moment then suddenly snapped back into focus, raising his voice. 'Now, I can't believe you fucking pains in the arse are still standing here talking and not dead.'

He lifted the gun and pointed it straight at Adam.

'You first, I think,' he said to Adam, then nodded at Roddy. 'Bigmouth next.' He turned to look at Molly. 'Then it has to be you, love. Sorry, but there's nothing I can do.'

'You're not sorry in the slightest,' said Molly.

Adam stared at the gun barrel pointing at him and felt faint. All the blood in his body seemed to pump into his head, which felt like it was about to explode. A raging gush filled his ears as he stood, unable to move. He watched Joe's finger begin to squeeze the trigger. It seemed to be happening excruciatingly slowly. Then he saw movement out of the corner of his eye. To begin with his brain couldn't work out what it was.

Suddenly a flood of clear liquid was spraying all over Joe and the gun, soaking him and making him screw up his eyes. He clawed at his eyeballs and the gun went off, the bullet close enough to Adam's head that he felt the wobble of air past his ear.

Adam heard a voice screaming at him and turned to see Roddy shouting, but couldn't work out what he was saying.

Roddy was pointing at Adam's hands. He looked down and saw he was still holding the blowtorch. Roddy waved the moonshine canister at him, showing him it was empty. That's what he'd thrown in Joe's face. Seventy per cent alcohol right in his eyes.

Adam's fingers fumbled as he tried to turn the gas nozzle of the blowtorch, eventually hearing the hiss. He looked at Joe, who was righting himself and opening his eyes, red raw and tear-stained. Adam clicked the ignition and heard the soft whoosh of blue flame in his hands. He lifted the blowtorch over his head and hurled it at Joe, whose eyes just had time to focus on the swirling blue flicker heading straight towards his doused head.

Joe ducked but it was too late, the body of the blowtorch hitting him on the cheek, the flame igniting his head in a sucking whump of sound, his whole upper body engulfed in flicking blue and orange heat that Adam could feel on his own face from a few yards away.

Adam stepped back as Joe staggered screaming towards them, gun waving around. The gun went off and they all scattered, then it went off again and again as Joe stumbled into the table, knocking chairs flying and clawing at the burning flesh of his face. The fire spread downwards until his whole body was bathed in persistent, consuming flames, the rancid smell of it making Adam retch.

The gun went off two more times as Joe staggered desperately towards the door, collapsing onto his knees and dropping the gun, his arms still flailing around. He slumped sideways onto the ground and began rolling backwards and forwards but the flames kept hold, turning his clothes and skin to a charred and bloody mess. Eventually he stopped rolling, and his arms fell to his side, but the flame kept burning, reluctant to give up such a willing host.

The three of them watched as Joe burned. Molly ran up and kicked the gun away from the body. She backed off and they stood, unable to speak, wary in case something insane happened like Joe suddenly springing back to life. It took five minutes for the fire to burn itself out, during which the three of them stared intensely at the flames, the blackened lump of flesh and exposed bone beneath. They covered their noses from the sickening stench.

Eventually Roddy spoke. 'Fuck me.'

'Is he definitely dead?' said Adam.

Molly walked over and looked impassively at the burnt-out corpse. She lifted a boot and kicked him hard in the face, bits of crispy, charred flesh flying free.

'He's dead, all right.'

30

Adam stood over Joe's body, pointing the gun at the blackened and deformed face. His hand was shaking. He gripped the gun in both hands but it still trembled.

'This is for Luke, you fucking cunt.'

'Stop!' shouted Molly, knocking his arm as he pulled the trigger.

The bullet ricocheted off the concrete floor and zipped past Roddy, who flinched.

'Jesus fucking Christ,' said Roddy. 'Watch it, for fuck's sake.'

Adam looked at Molly, confused, the gun limp at his side.

'I just wanted to . . .'

Molly shook her head.

'I thought you'd understand,' said Adam. 'After what he did to you.'

Molly frowned at him. 'We have to think clearly. We don't want to leave any evidence.'

'Evidence of what?' said Roddy, tooting more charlie from his case.

'That we were here.'

Roddy laughed and looked round at the carnage. 'It's a bit late for that, don't you think?'

'Not necessarily. If we leave a bullet in Joe's body, then it's obviously murder. If he just burned to death, it could be an accident. We have to think about the situation we're in here.'

'What situation?' said Roddy, sniffing. 'We take the police car and fuck off out of here sharp.'

'And go where?'

'Fucking anywhere.'

'It's a police car.'

'So?'

'So how do we explain that we're driving a police car?'

'What does it fucking matter?' Roddy swayed and sat down on the floor, clutching at his shoulder.

'We have two dead policemen on our hands. We can't be seen just driving their car around the island.'

Adam shook his head. 'But Grant was an accident and Joe was self-defence.'

'You think people are going to believe that if they catch us joyriding their squad car?'

'OK,' said Roddy. 'So we take the car and go see that old guy Eric you talked about. Tell him what's happened, let him sort it out.'

Molly considered this for a moment. 'Just because he's not involved, doesn't mean he'll be able to make this go away.'

'All right, then,' said Roddy. 'We take the car and drive to the outskirts of Port Ellen, then dump it and walk into town.'

Molly narrowed her eyes as she thought about this, then walked over to Joe's smouldering corpse. Thin trails of acrid smoke drifted from the body. She knelt down and tentatively touched his melted jacket pocket with the back of her hand. She held the pocket open with fingertips and moved her hand in carefully. She found something and snatched it out, muttering under her breath at the burning sensation in her hands. She dropped the item on the floor, shaking her hand. It was

Joe's car key, the plastic moulding melted all over the metal ridge of the key.

'That's that,' she said.

She went over to Grant's body and searched through his pockets.

'Nothing.' She looked at Adam and Roddy. 'Either of you two geniuses know how to hot-wire a car?'

'I skipped that class at uni,' said Roddy.

Adam just shook his head.

Molly got off her haunches with a sigh. 'Well, it looks like taking the car is a non-starter.'

She walked over to them. 'OK, let's think about this.' She seemed to be talking to herself more than them. 'We're in an illegal still with two dead policemen. We know other cops are involved in this operation, but we don't know whether they're from the island or the mainland. We have no idea how far this reaches. There are others coming soon to pick up a delivery in a boat.' She looked over at Joe's corpse, at the radio on his belt. 'We can't use the police radio, even if it wasn't melted, because they'll almost certainly be listening in.'

Silence for a moment, just the quiet thrum of machinery.

'So what do we do?' said Adam.

Molly gave a tight smile.

'I think there's a way out of this.'

Adam looked around. 'How? When they find this unholy mess, they'll come after us.'

Molly looked at him. 'Not if they don't know we ever existed.'

He was numb and exhausted, his brain frozen mush, but Adam began to see what she was getting at.

'Joe didn't mention us to them, did he?' he said.

'Not as far as we know.'

'So . . .' His mind stalled. 'So what are you saying, exactly?'

Molly took a deep breath. 'OK, here's how I see it. We have two dead cops, both burnt to death. So far, no bullet wounds.' She looked at the gun in Adam's hand. 'We have more dodgy cops on the way who probably don't know about us. So, we remove all trace of ourselves, set fire to the whole place, then when they arrive, all they find is a tragic accident, one they won't report because it involves implicating themselves in an illegal operation. A dangerous illegal operation, making the accidental fire all the more plausible.'

'But won't they see our tracks in the snow?' said Adam.

'Not if we don't give them reason to look for tracks,' said Molly. 'And if we're careful.'

'So how do we get back to civilisation?' said Roddy.

Molly considered this for a moment. 'We have to go back to the Audi and wait to be found.'

'What?' said Adam.

'It's the only way,' said Molly. 'And we have to take Luke's body with us.'

'Wait a minute,' said Roddy. 'Apart from the logistics of carting a dead body miles around the coast at night, he's got a bullet in his head and half his skull missing where Joe took a hammer to it. How do we explain that?'

Molly shrugged. 'We have to take him with us. He can't be found here, otherwise the whole thing is a bust.'

'OK,' said Roddy, 'we have to take him, but what about his head?'

Adam glimpsed over at Luke and felt sick. 'The skull

182

damage could've happened if he was thrown from the car. It doesn't look too different to what happened to Ethan.'

'And the bullet?'

Adam rubbed his forehead. 'We could set fire to the Audi with his body inside, maybe?'

'Come on,' said Roddy. 'You guys have seen *CSI*, right?'

'That's a television programme, Roddy, this is real fucking life here.'

Molly nodded to herself. 'Roddy's right, we have to get the bullet out.'

'What?' said Adam. 'How?'

'We'll cross that bridge when we come to it,' said Molly, looking at her watch. 'First, we have to get on with torching this place before those dodgy bastards arrive.'

She surveyed the scene. Roddy sat panting on the floor, washed-out and ill-looking.

'You up to trekking back to the car?' she asked.

'You saying I'm some kind of poof?' he grinned. 'Course I'm up to it. Think a tiny wee nick like this is going to bother me?' He looked at his injured shoulder and rocked a little.

Molly and Adam stared at him. He didn't look at all well, his forehead a sheen of sweat, face deathly grey, hands trembling.

Molly turned to Adam. 'You get Luke out of here, I'll start emptying those whisky casks all over the place. That should get a nice wee fire going. Reckon you could give me a hand, Roddy?'

He smiled thinly. 'Anything for a lady.'

Molly pointed at the floor next to the casks, where the contents of their pockets were still strewn across the ground. 'And we'll need to take all our stuff with us, obviously.'

Molly helped Roddy up and the three of them walked over and stuffed their belongings back in their pockets. Molly and Roddy then began pulling out the barrel plugs and tipping the hogsheads and butts over. Moonshine glugged and splashed out everywhere, and they rolled the casks around, spreading the liquid which spilled and pooled, filling the air with the sharp smack of alcohol.

Adam went over to Luke. He rubbed his hands up and down his face, wishing the image in front of him would disappear, but Luke was still lying there when he opened his eyes again.

'Fuck it,' he said under his breath, then grabbed Luke's ankles. He began pulling the body across the floor, but it was incredibly hard work, much tougher than he'd expected. Dead bodies weighed a fucking ton. He had to stop every few steps to get his breath back, feeling his aching muscles and stretching sinews. He slowly dragged Luke along in fits and starts, leaving a smeared, viscous trail of blood slewing through the spreading pools of whisky on the ground.

In the doorway, Molly was shaking a small cask so that moonshine splashed out onto the door and the floor.

'I hate to tell you this,' said Adam, 'but it's going to be murder carrying Luke's body back to the crash site. I can hardly move him.'

Molly took Luke's ankles and yanked, budging the body a few inches.

'Jesus, I see what you mean.' She looked outside. 'But we've got to get him out of here, and we can't have blood trails in the snow. Take his arms, we'll carry him together up the lane where the car tracks have flattened the snow, so we don't leave any footprints, then cut off to the right, back behind those rocks over there.'

They took the weight between them and stumbled and trudged uncertainly up the lane. It was hard work and they almost dropped him twice, only just catching a leg in time. They stayed on the lane as far as possible, until they were some distance from the barn, then staggered off behind an outcrop of rocks a couple of hundred yards away. They dumped the body with grunts and sighs, then got their breath back. Pale-faced in the moonlight and lying in a snowdrift, Luke seemed so comfortable. Adam felt tears come to his eyes and wiped them away.

'There's no bloody way we can carry him all the way back to the Audi,' said Adam.

'You're right.'

Adam looked at her in the moonlight, clear-eyed and bright. Their breaths were billowing around their heads.

'So what do we do?'

Molly looked back at the barn. 'I have an idea, leave it to me. Now, let's get that barn burned.'

They walked back down the lane and into the barn, then each rolled a cask outside, pushing them round the building, their open plugholes spilling whisky all over the walls.

When they'd finished, Molly rolled her empty cask back inside the still as Roddy came out. Adam went to copy her, but Molly stopped him. She went inside and came back out carrying the blowtorch and the claw hammer. She stuck the hammer in the plughole of the empty cask and yanked as hard as she could until the whole lid popped out with a creak of splintering wood. She threw the lid and the hammer back in through the open door and picked up the blowtorch.

Roddy looked confused. 'What do we need an empty barrel for?'

'You'll see,' said Molly.

Adam realised what she had in mind and shook his head in grim amazement.

She smiled at him. 'It'll work, trust me.'

'What will?' said Roddy.

'Never mind,' said Molly, lifting the blowtorch. 'Who wants to do the honours?'

They both shrugged, so she lit the torch, stepped forward and pointed it at the bottom of the entrance. The doors immediately erupted into flames, flickering tongues licking skywards. They all took a couple of steps back. The fire quickly spread round the oak walls of the barn and inside the door, they could already feel a fierce heat coming from it. Molly looked back at them for a moment, then turned and tossed the blowtorch far into the middle of the barn, where it instantly ignited into ferocious waves of flames. They felt air being sucked past them into the barn to fuel the inferno, as the noises of crackling fire and blistering wood rose in their ears.

They stood watching for a few moments as the fire spread through the barn, flames raging around the stills and the dead bodies, rolling over the barrels and casks, smoke swirling and billowing up towards the ceiling.

Molly examined the ground around them. It was a mess of slushy snow. Hopefully Joe and Grant's comings and goings, the police car's turning tracks and their own endeavours amounted to a slop of indistinguishable confusion.

'Come on,' said Molly, turning to Adam and slapping the empty barrel. 'Help me carry this up the lane, and make sure to keep your feet in the flattened car tracks.'

They lugged the barrel up the lane, Roddy close behind, the fire crackling loudly at their backs.

31

They headed up the path as far as Luke's body and turned to stare at the inferno. Flames were already licking the roof, flicking through huge clouds of acrid smoke pummelling up into the moonlit sky. One of the walls looked close to collapsing, and parts of the wooden roof were beginning to crack and fall into the raging fire beneath.

As they watched, a noise rose above the whoosh and crackle of the flaming barn, the nasal whine of an engine. Suddenly a large speedboat with police insignia spurted round the headland in a spray of water.

'Shit,' Molly hissed, 'help me with this.'

Adam took the opposite end of the barrel from Molly and they scurried behind the outcrop of rocks, Roddy slumping down next to Luke's body. They sat there for a while before Adam crept up to peek over the top.

The speedboat had docked in the tiny bay below the headland, and half a dozen men in dark uniform were scrambling up towards the barn in a fluster. Adam instinctively lowered his head, but they were a long way from the barn in the dark. There was no way they'd see him, surely.

The men reached the barn and were instantly rebuffed by the flames and heat bursting out the entrance. One of them did a quick circuit of the building while another bustled over to the police car, peered through the window then checked the driver's door, which was locked.

Adam saw a third man, arm held in front of his face as he stood looking at the collapsed entrance to the burning still. He lifted a police radio out of his belt and spoke into it. After a moment he looked at the radio as if it was malfunctioning. The other three men started a slow, methodical sweep around the immediate vicinity of the barn, searching with torches. One walked past the police car and began up the path towards them, making Adam duck back down next to Molly and Roddy.

'Shit,' he said. 'They're searching the area.'

They sat with their hearts thumping, not daring to move, Adam suddenly aware of the sound of his lungs pumping air. The cop was close enough now that they could hear the scrunch of his footsteps on the path and his laboured breathing as he headed up the slope. They were hidden from the lower part of the road, but they could tell from the noise that he'd stopped almost level with them. If he kept up the slope a few more yards and looked right, they'd be in plain view. They saw a torch beam sweep over the snow be-yond them and held their breaths. In the torchlight, Adam was relieved to see the police car's tracks had flattened the snow cover enough that they hadn't left footprints. He felt a wash of relief that they'd carried Luke's body, and that they'd lifted the barrel up the path and behind the rocks – Molly had made the right decision every time.

He looked at her now and she stared back at him, eyes wide. She moved her shoulders a fraction, a signal he couldn't decode. Then his gaze fell on her hands, and he realised she was holding Joe's pistol. He frowned at her and she frowned back, giving a kind of desperate shrug. They sat like that for what seemed an eternity as the beam from the torch played over the surrounding snowscape.

Eventually they heard footsteps again, this time moving back down the hill, getting quieter with every footfall until finally they were out of earshot.

Molly peered round the side of the rock. She didn't move or speak for a long time. After a while she turned round.

'He's back down with the others,' she said.

'You were going to shoot him?' said Adam.

'I don't know what the hell I was going to do, OK?' Molly glared at him. 'I'm just trying to stay alive here.'

'Sorry.'

Adam closed his eyes and tried to get his pulse to slow down. He opened his eyes again and looked at Roddy, whose gaze seemed to be going in and out of focus.

'You OK?'

Roddy blinked and smiled. 'Fucking dandy. What's the latest?'

Adam poked his head back up.

The men were standing arguing next to the burning building. There was a lot of gesticulating, towards the barn, then the police car, then the boat. Adam tried to second-guess what they might do, but didn't know where to start. The conversation went on for several minutes, lots of shaking heads and hand gestures, then eventually they seemed to take a vote, four of the six men putting their hands up.

They headed towards the police car. The man in front pulled out his baton and nonchalantly smashed in the driver's window, then opened the door and leaned in while the others started pushing. The car began to crawl down the gentle slope, gradually picking up speed as it passed the barn, the men jogging alongside or still shoving from behind. It was heading for the edge of a short drop, the tiny natural harbour of the bay below, the speedboat anchored safely off to one side.

As they approached the edge the man guiding the steering wheel let go and moved out of the way, the rest of them giving up on pushing as the car gently freewheeled over the edge and bounced boot over bonnet into the water with a resigned splash.

The men stood at the edge of the bay, gazing at the water as the car slipped under the surface. It must be deeper than it looked because soon all trace of the car was gone, just a spreading moonlit ripple on the inky surface of the sea.

The men turned back to look at the barn, which was shapeless now, a giant funeral pyre raging into the night sky. As they watched there was an almighty explosion from within it, making them and Adam jump as pieces of burning wreckage shot outwards and upwards from the inferno, flames stretching up with the force of the blast.

'What the fuck was that?' hissed Roddy from behind the rock.

Adam turned and shrugged. 'Explosion.'

'Probably the second still going,' said Molly. 'I turned all the dials on it full up before we left. Figured it wouldn't hurt.'

Adam smiled and looked at the gang of coppers, who were now heading back to the speedboat, eager to get the hell out of there and away from the incriminating evidence.

Another small explosion made them all flinch, then stop and stare, before scurrying and clambering into the boat which lurched round and away from the bay in a flurry of white surf and revs.

Molly joined Adam to watch as the boat sped round the headland and out of sight. They stood looking at the burning still and the undulating water for a while.

Adam turned to her. 'You know, I didn't even know Scottish police had speedboats.'

Molly smiled. 'Just like *Miami Vice*, huh?'

'What now?' he said.

Molly looked behind them at Luke's body and the empty barrel. Roddy was sat next to it, eyes closed, his face set in a grimace, clutching at his bloody shoulder. She walked over to the barrel and stood it on its end.

'Help me get him inside, then,' she said, indicating Luke.

Adam sighed then joined her, taking Luke's legs as she heaved under his armpits.

Roddy's eyes flickered open. 'What the fuck are you two doing?'

Adam lugged the legs up and over the rim of the cask and began sliding them in, moving his hands up Luke's body to help Molly lift the other end high enough. 'Isn't it bloody obvious?'

'OK, but why?'

Molly gave a grunt of exertion as she got her body weight under Luke's back. 'He's too heavy to carry, and we have to take him with us.'

She and Adam were slowly shuffling the corpse into the barrel in fits and starts.

'In a fucking barrel?' said Roddy.

'Yes,' said Molly. 'In a barrel.'

The body slumped over the edge and fell into the cask. They tucked his arms in and Molly gently eased his shoulders and neck until his head was completely inside.

'It's a snug fit,' said Adam, getting his breath back.

'Probably just as well, don't want him rattling around in there, or falling out.'

Roddy looked at them breathing heavily next to the barrel. 'You two are priceless.'

Adam just stared at him as his breath returned to normal.

'Right,' said Molly, rubbing her hands together to warm them up. 'Time to head back to the car and get ourselves saved.'

32

It was incredibly slow going. They had to stop every fifty yards so that Roddy could rest and try to get some energy back. Each time he would take a hit of coke, fuelling him with bullshit strength to carry on for a few minutes more. Molly and Adam were glad of each rest stop anyway. They were rolling the barrel along together, and although it was ten times easier than carrying the body had been, it was still a hard slog. The terrain was the biggest problem. When they had some semblance of a path it was fine, but they frequently had to negotiate rocks, scrub and deep shingle, where they would have to lift or jostle the barrel over or around the obstacle before ploughing grimly on.

It was dark again, the moon crowded out by gangs of clouds. Roddy was in front with the torch, splaying the beam over the land and trying to find the best way to take the barrel. The torch and Joe's handgun were the only things they'd brought with them from the still apart from the barrel. The plan was to throw all three items into the sea once they got to the car. The last thing they needed was to have police paraphernalia or anything linked to the still on them when they were rescued.

Roddy staggered across the land, getting slower and slower. They were stopping more frequently now, every few yards, exhausted from the trek and everything that had gone before.

Adam felt the cold settling into his bones again after the heat of the still, his soaking feet numb, his hands stiffening. The adrenalin from escaping Joe had dissipated and he was left with a miserable empty feeling, exacerbated by catching occasional glimpses of the crown of Luke's head bobbing at the open end of the cask. He resorted to putting one foot in front of the other like a machine, trying not to think of anything except getting out of this situation in one piece.

Suddenly they heard a nasal whine. It grew louder, encroached on the thick silence of the night around them. They stopped and looked at each other.

'Torch,' Molly hissed, glaring at Roddy.

He flicked it off just as the police speedboat from earlier fizzed round the headland, close to the shore. It had a large searchlight mounted on the front, sweeping its beam along the coastline, back and forth over rocks and cliffs. The three of them stood for a second, frozen, then darted behind the cask. Adam was confused – had they had that searchlight before, just not used it? He couldn't remember seeing it, but that didn't mean anything, his mind was worn out with it all.

The three of them and the barrel were quite far inland, a spread of jagged boulders between them and the sea, maybe far enough away that they wouldn't be spotted. The searchlight arced past them higher up the slope, then swept back lower down, rippling over the rocks below, then moving further on. Adam could hear himself breathe heavily as the sound of the boat's engine receded, then it was gone past the next headland.

'Why are they looking for us?' said Adam. 'I thought we'd left no trace.'

'Calm down,' said Molly. 'We don't know they're looking

for us specifically, do we?'

'Then what the fuck are they searching the coast for?' said Roddy.

'Maybe just making sure,' said Molly. 'If you were a cop and you were running a big bootlegging operation that went tits up, wouldn't you want to make sure there were no potential witnesses in the area?'

'But why would they think there were any witnesses?' said Adam.

'I don't know, OK?' Molly snapped. 'Like I just said, maybe they don't know anything. One thing's for sure, if they see us we're screwed, so let's just be extra careful from now on.'

They trudged on, nervy and exhausted, Adam swithering between numb desolation and flurried panic attacks, unable to stop his mind churning over events, everything that had happened, all the potential pitfalls that still waited for them round every corner.

Finally, drained of all emotion and energy, they reached the headland before the crashed car. They scuffed round in silence, Molly and Adam still heaving the cask in front of them with worn-out shoves, Roddy staggering uncertainly with every step. They stopped when they caught sight of the Audi. It was almost submerged in water, just the wheels and undercarriage poking up through the waves.

Adam tried to think about tides. There were two a day, right? How long had they been away? What time was it now anyway? He thought he could detect a lightening in the sky in the east, the black grading to purple at the edge of the horizon, and distant clouds brightening a little.

They picked up the pace, urged on by the sight of the car,

still casting nervous glances out to sea. There was no sign of the police boat, just the slick undulations of the vast expanse of water stretching to infinity.

They finally slumped exhausted just uphill from the car, Roddy easing himself down to lie flat out on the snow-covered grass, Molly and Adam heaving the barrel onto its end next to Ethan's body. The sight of Ethan brought everything back to Adam, the sick feeling in his gut, the terrible guilt. He felt rage bubble up inside him, but was too weak to do anything about it.

He slumped down onto the ground next to Roddy and put his head on the cold land. The clouds above him seemed to whirl round in a complicated dance, and he felt sick and disoriented looking at them.

He tried to take deliberate breaths, stop the nausea, but he felt bile rise in his gut. He sat up just in time to puke, angling his head to the side but still dribbling down his clothes. The vomit left a taste of bitter moonshine in his mouth, reminding him of the still and everything that had happened there. He sat panting and spitting for a while, then grabbed a handful of snow and washed his mouth out with it.

He looked up at the cliff towering over them. It was insane to think they had driven off that ledge and crumpled underneath less than twenty-four hours ago. This time yesterday he'd been sitting in Molly's flat in Port Ellen drinking her thirty-year-old and talking quietly, sharing that one clumsy, tender kiss. He couldn't imagine ever kissing her again.

She was gazing at the Audi, playing with the torch Roddy had dumped, deep in her own thoughts. In one way he felt closer to her than anyone else in the world now, but the shared experience was a barrier as well – they would always remind each other of this nightmare.

And anyway, it wasn't over yet, not by a long way.

He looked at the car. The tide was receding; there was more of the undercarriage showing and now part of the boot as well. He was distracted by Roddy coughing violently, his body convulsing with the force of it. He put a hand on Roddy's chest and felt his breath rattling. His whole right side was soaked in blood, his face totally white now, ghostly.

'We need to get help soon,' said Molly, looking at Roddy.

'Roddy?' said Adam.

Roddy opened his eyes and a faint smile appeared on his blue lips. He winked slowly.

'I wouldn't go to sleep if I were you,' said Adam. 'You might not wake up again.'

Roddy coughed.

'Fuck you,' he croaked. 'You're not getting rid of me that easily.'

'So,' said Adam, turning to Molly. 'It feels like I'm always saying this, but what do we do now?'

She sighed, got up, walked over to the barrel and put one hand on the rim.

'The bullet in Luke's head. We have to get it out.'

'Jesus.'

'Yeah.' She carefully tipped the barrel over onto its side and sat down, bracing her legs against the rim. 'Help me get him out, then.'

Adam sat next to her and took one of Luke's arms as she took the other. They both pulled, leaning back, pushing their legs against the barrel to prise him free. A handful of heaves and he was out.

They rolled him onto his back, then peered into the mess at the side of his head, Adam feeling his stomach clench at the sight. There was a mash of skull fragments, brains, blood and matted hair.

'Are we sure the bullet's definitely still in there?' said Adam, turning away.

'That's what Joe thought, anyway.'

'Maybe it worked its way out on the trip back here.'

Molly smiled a joyless smile. 'Wishful thinking.'

'So what do we do?'

Molly dragged her hands down her face in a tired movement and looked at him. 'Get it out.'

'How?'

'How do you think?'

Adam stared at her. 'You've got to be kidding.'

Molly raised her eyebrows and shrugged.

'We can't leave the bullet in there,' she said. 'It ties us to Joe, Grant and the still. You know that.'

Eventually Adam nodded. 'I know.'

'One of us has to get in there and get the bullet out.'

Adam stared at Molly, then glanced at the mess of Luke's head. He looked away as he felt his mouth start to sweat. Luke was his friend. It was his fault they were in this mess, his fault Luke was dead. It was his responsibility.

33

Nothing could've prepared him for the gut-wrenching, visceral sickness of this.

Of course he'd seen autopsies on television dramas, but those were sterilised, one step removed from reality.

They'd searched their pockets for a useful implement, but all they came up with was a pen of Molly's. Adam cursed their stupidity for not bringing tools from the still.

He took a deep breath and began tentatively poking into the gaping wound in Luke's head with the pen, his trembling hands making it impossible to control it with any precision. There was a deep fluttering in his stomach, teetering on the brink of vomiting at any minute.

At least a quarter of Luke's head was smashed in where Joe had hacked away at it, one side of the face a hash of minced flesh and broken bone, the eye just a sticky mess of creamy mucus. The surrounding hair was matted and thick with blood, the ear completely missing, or in there but unrecognisable, the whole thing a shiny red-and-black hellhole of flesh.

Molly pointed the torch at the wound but looked away. Adam heard a faint squelching sound as he pushed some purple material aside, a chunk of something fleshy falling out. His stomach lurched and he coughed stinging bile onto the snow to his side. He wiped his mouth on his sleeve and looked back at the wound.

Molly's torch beam had moved, so he positioned her hand again. He stuck the pen in, unsure what the hell he was even looking for, why the fuck he was doing this. He lifted a flap of something out of the way and saw sickly grey jelly oozing out from underneath. The brain. Everything that made Luke who he was, or had been, was in that gruesome lump of soft putty. He caught a faint whiff of a smell, like something rotting in the back of the fridge, and he gagged, retching again into the snow as he turned from the mess of Luke's head.

'Want me to do it?' said Molly.

He shook his head and turned back. He forced himself to poke about in the gaping maw, moving loose bits aside, flicking under and into crevices, trying to work out where a bullet might be, if it was in there at all. But it had to still be in there, didn't it? That's what had puzzled Joe back at the still, there was no exit wound. Adam knew from Luke's scar that the metal plate was somewhere round the back of his head, did that mean the bullet was in the same area? Or could it have ricocheted back inside his skull?

Adam was getting frustrated, digging deeper and deeper into the flesh and muscle and skull and brains and finding nothing. He could feel sweat cooling and freezing on his brow. His stomach had got used to what he was doing, but his mind hadn't. He would see this image every night while he slept for the rest of his life. Luke's open head would haunt him into eternity.

He couldn't find anything. Maybe the bullet had made it out after all. Or maybe it was buried deep in the middle of the brain, or stuck in the skull somewhere, or lodged in the metal plate at the other side. He pushed the pen in almost as far as it would go, then felt a gentle clunk as it tapped the metal plate. He pulled it out and examined it, several inches of slime and blood down its length. He was fucked if he was going to dig that deep into Luke's consciousness. But maybe he would have to. He started again in the debris he could see, gradually sweeping through the layers of fleshy mess. He saw something glimmer amongst the carnage, something metallic.

'Hold the torch closer,' he said, moving Molly's wrist again. 'I've found something.'

Molly glanced at the wound then looked away. 'The bullet?'

'I think so.'

He stuck the pen in. To reach it, he had to rest his hands against the cold, bloody flesh of the wound, holding the pen in both hands to try to keep it steady. A shudder went through his body as he touched Luke's raw flesh. He flicked at the object with the pen but it didn't budge. He leaned in further and tried again, but it still wouldn't move. He tried a third time and the thing slipped further into the surrounding grey matter, so that only the very end was visible.

'Shit.'

'What?'

'It's fucking slippery.' He turned to Molly. 'I'm going to have to get it with my fingers.'

Molly closed her eyes and Adam turned back. He took a deep breath. Serenity now.

'Wish me luck.'

'Good luck.'

Grimacing, he reached in and began scraping flesh and brain out of the way. It felt like raw mince, but he kept going. He reached for the object lodged in the brain but it slipped from his shaking hands, burying itself deeper into the mess. He grabbed a handful of brain and ripped it out of the way, wiping his hand on the adjacent eye socket. The object was exposed. He reached back in and dug it out, getting brain under his fingernails, his stomach now spasm after spasm, his eyes watering, his forehead sweating, his whole body shivering with the cold and the stress and the repulsive truth of what he was doing.

He lifted it out and held it up.

'Thank fuck,' he said, showing the bullet to Molly.

'Jesus,' she said. 'Well done.'

He stared at the bloody mess of his hands.

'What now?'

Molly looked along the coast, Adam's eyes following. It was definitely getting close to dawn, the sky light in the east now. It looked like it might be a nice day.

'Throw it in the sea,' said Molly. 'But not here, along the coast a bit. And make sure it goes further than low tide.'

'How do I know where low tide is?'

Molly shrugged. 'Just throw it as far as you can.'

Adam eased himself up, holding the bullet between his fingers like a gemstone. He began walking away to the east.

'And don't forget to wash your hands,' Molly said after him.

He walked a couple of hundred yards and stopped. He looked at the bullet. Such a tiny thing to kill someone. Such a minuscule thing to end a life, to change everything so irrevocably, to put an end to someone's hopes and dreams and everything in their future.

He held it tight in his palm then launched it into the sea, watching as it arced through the pinkish sky and landed with a gentle plop, breaking the surface of the perfectly calm black water.

He bent down at the water's edge and began rubbing his hands together in the wash. The water was shockingly cold, his fingers numb, but he could still feel the small specks of grit under his nails, reminders of Luke's life. He laughed bitterly to himself as he scrubbed at his fingers and palms, scratching at the skin with his nails until his hands were raw and sore. He felt pain as he scraped away, and it felt like sweet relief.

He walked back.

Roddy was out cold. He had Ethan's jacket over him as a blanket.

'He OK?' said Adam.

Molly nodded. 'Just checked. His pulse is a bit shallow, but he's still breathing fine.'

They both turned to Luke, Molly playing the torch beam over his head. It was an unholy mess.

'Think it looks like a gunshot wound?' she said.

Adam stared at it. 'I have no idea. A shotgun, maybe. What do you think?'

Molly shrugged. 'We shouldn't take the chance.'

Adam turned to her. 'What do you mean?'

'You've seen the forensic stuff on telly. I know it's probably bullshit, but they might still be able to tell he was shot.'

'So what can we do?'

Molly looked out at the implacable spread of water. 'I think we should throw him in the sea.'

'What?'

'If they examine the body now, they might find gunshot residue or something, I don't know. But if it spends a couple of days in open water getting nibbled by fish and seagulls, maybe they won't be able to detect anything. Deterioration of evidence, something like that.'

'Do you have any idea what you're talking about?'

Molly stared at him. 'Not really, but don't you think it's worth trying?'

Adam sat down, utterly exhausted. 'To be honest, I don't give a shit any more. What does it matter if we're connected with Joe? Our lives are fucking meaningless now anyway. How are we supposed to go on after all this?'

He waved his arm around aimlessly.

'You don't mean that,' said Molly.

'I do.'

Molly sat down next to him. 'Do you want to spend the rest of your life in jail for murdering two cops?'

'But if we just tell the truth . . .'

'It's too late for the truth. Forget about the truth.'

Adam examined his fingers closely. It felt like he still had something under his fingernails, but when he dug into them he found nothing. He spotted a small, dark fleck of something on his finger. He peered at it. It was the skelf he got from the cask at Laphroaig, when Molly gave them the tour. He prodded it, feeling a slight twinge under the skin.

'Forget about the truth?' he said quietly.

'Yes.'

He hauled himself up with immense tiredness, his entire body aching beyond words, his mind blank.

'Come on then,' he said. 'Let's throw Luke in the sea.'

34

'Wake up.'

Adam shook Roddy, gently at first, then harder when he didn't respond.

'Wake up.'

He felt Roddy's neck. For a moment, all Adam could feel was his frozen fingers pressing against warm flesh, then he thought he detected something. A faint pulse, slowing and speeding up haphazardly, leaping all over the place.

'Roddy!'

He removed Ethan's jacket from him and grabbed the front of Roddy's coat, lifting him up and shaking him.

'Fucking Jesus,' said Roddy, his eyes snapping open, his hand reaching for his shoulder. 'What the fuck are you doing?'

Adam let go, not realising Roddy wasn't supporting himself. Roddy slumped to the ground with a thud.

'Fucking hell, Strachan, you trying to kill me?'

'Sorry,' said Adam. 'I panicked. I thought you were dying.'

Roddy smiled and winced. 'Wouldn't give you the satisfaction.'

'Don't be a dickhead all your life,' said Adam.

'Hey, gorgeous,' said Roddy as Molly appeared. 'I'm in need of some TLC here. Fancy it?'

His voice was weak and croaky, despite the bullshit.

Molly gave him a withering glare. 'We need to get our stories straight.' She looked around. 'When we get rescued.'

'If we get rescued, you mean,' said Adam.

Molly looked at him. 'I mean when. I'm not going through all this shit just to die here.'

Roddy struggled on his good elbow to sit up. 'Someone give me a fucking hand, eh?'

Adam lifted him to a sitting position and sat next to him. Molly stood over them, scanning the horizon. The sea was black glass.

Roddy tried to get something out of his jacket, grimacing.

'Help me out here,' he said, pointing at his pocket.

Adam delved in and pulled out the coke case. He looked at it.

'I can't believe you're still taking this shit,' he said.

Roddy grabbed it from him and opened it one-handed with practised skill. He lifted a mound out on his finger and snorted it, wiping the leftovers on his gums.

'Purely medicinal,' he said, licking his teeth and snorting again.

'Does coke even have any painkilling properties?'

Roddy stared at him. 'When you've got a fucking gaping wound in your shoulder with a piece of fucking metal sticking out of it, feel free to come back and ask me about pain relief, OK?'

He looked around.

'Where's Luke?'

Adam and Molly exchanged a glance.

'In the sea,' said Adam.

'Want to tell me why?' Roddy seemed immediately bolstered by the coke.

'We thought it was best,' said Molly.

'Why?'

'Adam got the bullet out, but . . .'

'Wait,' Roddy turned to Adam. 'You got the bullet out?'

Adam looked down. 'Yeah.'

'How?'

Adam stared at his hands, then lifted them and showed them to Roddy, waggling his fingers solemnly.

'Jesus,' said Roddy.

'Yeah.'

Molly cut in. 'Anyway, we didn't know if they could still tell it was a gunshot wound, so we dumped him in the sea, from that ledge over there.'

Roddy followed her finger.

'Couldn't we have just done that miles back, instead of rolling him all the way here in that thing?' He pointed at the barrel.

Molly looked out to sea again. 'We needed to get away from the still fast, didn't we? And we had to get the bullet out, remember. Anyway, it's better that we threw him in here, maybe some smart police bastard knows the tides in this area. If we'd thrown him in along the coast, he might have washed up somewhere that conflicts with our story. All we have to say now is that we have no idea where Luke is. He must've been thrown clear in the crash, all the way into the water. That could've happened.'

Roddy and Adam looked at each other.

'It could've,' insisted Molly.

'You sound like you've got it all worked out,' said Roddy.

'Not really,' said Molly. 'I'm just trying to think logically.'

'So what's the rest of our story?' said Roddy.

'Simple,' said Molly. 'We tell the truth about Ethan. We moved his body, but so what? And we just say that we've been here by the wreckage the whole time.'

Roddy shook his head. 'Why the fuck would we just sit here and do nothing all that time?'

'We just did, OK?' said Molly. 'When we came to, we searched around this area for Luke for a while, then we thought it best to stay with the vehicle and wait to be rescued. Maybe we thought it wasn't safe for you to move with your injury, you weren't up to it, and we didn't want anyone going off and looking for help alone.'

Roddy nodded. 'I suppose that makes sense.' He looked around. 'So how do we *actually* get rescued, then?'

Molly looked at the car. The tide was going out, the undercarriage and half the chassis now exposed.

'We need to start a fire, get some attention.'

She walked down to the car. The boot was above the waterline, so she leaned in and flipped the catch. It popped open downwards and a gush of seawater poured out along with a handful of bits and bobs which floated around in the gently lapping tide. She lifted a petrol canister from the debris in the water, then pushed herself away from the car. She turned to them, opened the canister and sniffed.

'Bingo. If we pour this over the undercarriage and tyres, strike a match, should make a pretty big smoke signal.'

Roddy pulled a lighter out of his pocket with a groan of pain.

'Go on then,' he said offering it. 'I could do with getting saved. I'm in fucking agony here.'

'Not so fast,' said Molly. 'We have to get rid of the barrel,

212

the gun and the torch first.'

Roddy looked out to sea. 'Shouldn't we keep the gun in case those bastards in the speedboat come back?'

Molly put the canister down and searched the horizon. The sky was light in the east now, high feathering clouds striping the sky.

'They won't come back,' she said. 'It was hours ago we saw them, they can't still be out on the water. Besides, it's almost daylight, they wouldn't risk it. They were probably just checking along the coastline until they ran short of fuel, then headed back to wherever the hell they came from.' She pulled the gun out from the back of her trousers. 'And we have to get rid of this, it is a murder weapon, after all.'

She put the gun back, picked up the torch and put it in her pocket, then stood next to the barrel and looked at Adam.

'Come on then, give me a hand with this thing.'

They headed off in the opposite direction to the one they'd taken Luke's body, rolling the barrel for several hundred yards until they reached a large rocky outcrop. Molly wiped the handles of the torch and the gun then hurled them both as hard as she could into the sea. They splashed into the surface with the quiet thunks of metal in water.

She turned to look at Adam.

'So we just roll this into the sea?' he said, looking at the barrel.

'I guess so.'

'It'll float.'

Molly shrugged. 'There are no markings on it, there's nothing to tie it to us or the still.'

'Won't there be some of Luke's blood in there?'

'The sea will take care of that.'

'You think?'

'I honestly have no idea, but it's our only option.'

They counted to three then heaved the barrel and watched as it tipped into the water below them, landing with a soft splash and bobbing around, bumping into the rocky coastline and slowly filling with water.

Adam rubbed his face and sighed, then looked at Molly. 'You really think this can work?'

Molly nodded. 'It can if we stick together.'

They walked back to the car, Adam feeling utterly empty, a lost soul.

Roddy lifted his head slowly as they approached.

'Sorted?'

They both nodded wearily.

'I've got another question,' he said. 'How do we explain that we didn't light a fire until now?'

Molly considered this for a moment. 'Who's to say we didn't? Maybe we started it last night, but no one was around to see it. We couldn't send up an inferno because we only had one little petrol canister, we had to ration it because we didn't know when we were going to be found.'

'And what makes you think someone is going to see the smoke now and come to the rescue?'

'Look, I never said the plan was perfect, did I?' said Molly, running a hand through her hair and down her neck. 'Do you want to try and get out of here alive or don't you?'

'Of course.'

'Well stop being the smart bastard picking holes in everything and start being helpful for once in your sorry little life.'

Roddy smiled at her. 'OK, take it easy. I'm just asking the questions the police are going to ask.'

Adam looked up. 'What do you mean?'

Roddy smiled at him. 'This all stinks to high fucking heaven. You think they're not going to give us a grilling?'

'But we're just innocent victims of a car crash, right?' said Adam.

'Who just happen to be stranded a few walkable miles along the coast from two dead cops and a burnt-out illegal still. In the middle of fucking nowhere. You think they're going to buy that it's a coincidence?'

'But they might not even find the still or the bodies,' said Adam weakly.

Roddy shook his head. 'They'll find them. Or at least we have to assume they will.'

'Roddy's right,' said Molly. 'We have to presume the worst, be prepared to get interrogated.'

'The interesting bit,' said Roddy, 'is gonna be whether the cops who interview us are in on the bootlegging operation or not.'

Adam put his head in his hands. 'Jesus Christ, this is never going to end, is it?'

Roddy coughed then smiled as he lay back down on the ground, cradling his shoulder in his hand.

'It'll end eventually,' said Molly. 'One way or the other.'

35

'What if no one comes?' said Adam.

Molly shrugged as she poured more petrol on the Audi's undercarriage. The flames roared briefly, sending thick black smoke billowing straight up into a pristine sky. The acrid stench of burning fuel and rubber filled their noses. She shoogled the canister and listened. It was half empty already. She put it down next to Roddy, passed out on the ground under Ethan's coat.

'Someone will come.'

Adam looked west, the direction of the still. There was no trace of smoke in the sky over there. Were they too far away to see it? Had it burnt out already? Had someone spotted it in the night and called the fire brigade to put it out? Did they even have a fire brigade on Islay?

'There's no smoke from the still,' he said.

'I know.'

'What does that mean?'

'I don't know.'

Adam looked back at their own smoke signal, reaching lazily upwards into the cold blue.

'What if no one comes?'

Molly turned to him. 'I don't have all the answers, I'm as much in the dark as you are. Stop asking stupid questions.'

Adam looked at her. She seemed close to tears, a wetness

in her eyes, but then it could've been the petrol fumes. She turned away from his gaze.

Adam looked out to sea, then turned back as he realised Molly was crying – thick, heavy sobs into her hands as her body convulsed with the release of it.

'It's OK,' he said, getting up and trying to put his arm around her. She flinched at his touch and shook him off.

'It's not OK,' she snapped. 'It's never going to be OK, what's happened.'

Adam stared at her back as she composed herself, wiping away tears with the backs of her hands and sniffing. He felt empty and didn't know what to say.

'Look, we're all just a bit stressed,' he said.

Molly laughed, a slice of acidic sound. 'You think?'

They looked at each other, something passing between them, a flicker of what they'd felt back at her place, maybe, a painful reminder of how their lives could've been.

'Sorry,' he said again.

'What do you have to be sorry for?'

'If it wasn't for me, none of us would be in this mess.'

Molly shook her head. 'We were unlucky, that's all.'

It was Adam's turn to laugh. 'I think unlucky is an understatement, don't you?'

'Maybe.'

He tentatively tried to put his arm round her again. To his surprise, she allowed herself to be held, leaning into him. He smelled her hair, a faint flowery shampoo amongst the bitter smokiness of the fire. It felt so nice holding her, he never wanted to let go. In the middle of the night, back in the still, he could never have imagined being this close to her again. He didn't want it to end.

She pulled away awkwardly and nodded at Roddy.

'Better check on numb-gums,' she said. 'Make sure he hasn't OD-ed.'

She knelt and took the wrist of his good arm, felt for his pulse. She nodded. 'Still with us, but weak. We should think about a Plan B for getting rescued quicker.'

'Like what?'

Molly shrugged again. 'Maybe one of us could walk round the coast the other way, see what we can find.'

'You think that's a good idea?'

'I really don't know.'

'Wait,' said Adam. 'You hear something?'

It was faint, but there was definitely a rattling chug in the air. As he strained to listen it got louder, the sound of a rough diesel engine clanking and rumbling away. It was coming from above, up on the road, although he couldn't see anything from down here.

Molly ran over and threw some more petrol on the fire, standing back as flames and smoke whooshed into the sky. They both turned, looking desperately along the top of the cliff where the road ran, and screaming. They were shouting and hollering for all they were worth as the engine noise grew louder and louder, then suddenly they saw a rusting tractor pulling up to the edge above them.

They were still yelling and now jumping up and down, waving their arms frantically as an old woman climbed out of the cab and peered down at them. She waved and they waved back.

'Are you all right?' Her voice was faint, with a thick island accent.

'We need help,' shouted Molly.

'Anyone injured?'

'One of us,' said Molly. 'We've got one dead as well, and one . . . missing.'

She looked at Adam on that last word.

'Heavens,' said the woman. 'Oh my goodness. Hang on, I'll get help. Can you wait? I need to go back to the farm to phone the police. That'll take half an hour, it's the other side of the Oa.'

Molly laughed. 'Half an hour is fine, thank you.'

'Not at all, my dear,' the woman said. 'Just hang on, we'll get you out of there in a jiffy.'

The woman disappeared into the tractor, which revved then crawled away. They listened as the engine noise receded, then looked at each other, grins breaking out on their faces. They quickly hugged each other, then separated clumsily.

'Thank Christ,' said Molly, smiling and shaking her head.

'I know.' Adam put his head in his hands. 'I can't believe it.'

'Come on,' said Molly. 'Let's tell Roddy we've saved his miserable wee life.'

They trudged over and slumped to their knees next to him.

'Roddy,' said Adam, shaking him. 'Come on, Roddy, wake up, we're saved.'

Roddy didn't move.

'Come on, big guy,' Adam whispered into his ear. 'Wake up, it's going to be OK.'

No response.

Adam put two fingers to Roddy's wrist, waited a moment, then pressed the fingers into his neck.

'I can't find a pulse.'

'What?' said Molly.

Adam put an ear to Roddy's mouth and a hand on his chest. 'Is he breathing?'

Adam shrugged, then grabbed Roddy's head and shook. 'Roddy, fucking hell.'

A smile crept over Roddy face as he opened his eyes, taking a while to focus.

'What are you cunts waking me up for?' he whispered. 'I was having a pretty sweet dream about an orgy.'

'Never mind that shit,' said Adam, breathing heavily. 'We've been spotted. We're going to be rescued. Some old dear is away to get help. The smoke signal worked.'

Roddy smiled weakly.

'Now it's going to get interesting,' he said. 'Pass me that fucking coke.'

36

Two hours later they were chugging along the coast in an RNLI lifeboat heading for Port Ellen. The old lady had phoned the police, a spotty young copper appearing after an hour, assessing the situation and realising he didn't have any equipment to get them back up the cliff. He called the lifeboat, which had to come from Port Askaig on the other side of the island, so it was almost noon by the time they were lugging Roddy and Ethan onto stretchers and helping Adam and Molly on board, Molly briefly swapping relieved banter with a member of the crew she knew.

They were given hot drinks and blankets, one of the crew injecting Roddy with morphine, another covering Ethan's body with a sheet, for all the good that would do. The sight of Ethan and Luke's mangled faces would always live with Adam, always haunt him.

They quickly gave the bare bones of their story to one of the crew, who listened impassively then went to radio it in to the police, contacting the ambulance at the same time to let them know what was coming.

Adam sat sipping from his cup, warming his hands, blanket hugged to his body. He felt strangely in limbo. The ordeal was over, they were rescued, but there was no relief, no possibility to relax. He and Molly still had a shitload of explaining to do. Or did they? Had anyone found Joe and Grant's bodies? And if they had, would the police suspect a connection?

He watched the coast drift by, rocky cliffs peppered with nests and populated by swooping seabirds. Just as well they hadn't tried to walk this way, there didn't seem to be any path along the coast in this direction. Then again, heading the other way had got them into the biggest heap of fucking trouble of their lives. Should've stayed put, done the smoke signal thing from the start, then Luke would still be alive. But would anyone have been around to see the smoke? Still, sitting there in the freezing cold for the night would've been better than what they'd gone through. Bloody hindsight. He was tearing himself up about it, unable to get the sight of Luke's missing face out of his head, the sound and smell of the wound, the feel of the cold flesh against his. It was unbearable. But he had to keep it together for all their sakes.

'You OK?' said Molly.

He shook his head, then felt her hand on his wrist.

He turned and smiled at her, but it was a weak gesture, a positivity he didn't feel, and it felt stupid and unconvincing on his face.

Molly looked past him.

'Here we go,' she said.

Adam turned to see the low whitewashed rows of Port Ellen.

'Back to civilisation, eh?' he said.

Molly laughed under her breath. 'Don't know if I'd call it that.'

The boat turned towards the gap in the harbour wall, and they sped through it, Adam spotting the B&B where they were all still checked in. Shit, he would have to take Ethan and Luke's stuff away. How long would Roddy be in hospital?

What if he needed treatment off the island? They didn't even have a car now, how would they ever get away from here? Maybe the police wouldn't let them get away.

He saw the ambulance waiting at the dockside, a single police car next to it. An old copper with a paunch stood drinking coffee and chatting to the ambulance driver and another man with a camera.

'Eric,' said Molly, pointing.

'Yeah?' said Adam. 'Should we tell him what really happened?'

Molly frowned to herself for a few moments. 'I don't think so.'

'I thought you said you trusted him.'

'I don't for a minute think he was in on the still operation, but that doesn't mean we should go blabbing everything to him. Like I said to Roddy, he's not Jim'll Fix It, just an old copper who happened to know my dad.'

'But maybe he can help.'

'Maybe we won't need any help. If we could've got a hold of him last night, maybe he would've come and got us, but we're rescued now, I don't know how much help he can be. Let's just stick to the story. We don't want to start telling different versions to different people, we're bound to trip ourselves up that way. Let's just wait and see what the police have found at the still, if they've found anything. If me, you and Roddy stick to our story and don't fuck it up, we won't be implicated in anything.'

'You really think so?'

Molly stared at him. 'Just stay calm. Don't start embellishing anything, just stick to the basic facts – we crashed, we found Ethan, we searched for Luke, we couldn't find him, we lit a fire, we got found in the morning. OK?'

'OK.'

Their boat pulled in alongside the dock and tied up, Adam and Molly thanking the crew profusely, words they waved away. Eric helped Molly then Adam out of the boat as the ambulance crew took Roddy and Ethan on stretchers into the back of their vehicle. The bloke with the camera began taking pictures of it all.

'Not now, Dean,' the policeman said, then turned to Molly. 'Sounds like you've been through the wringer, dear.'

'Hi, Eric,' said Molly. 'Yeah, quite something. Thought we'd never be found. This is Adam, by the way.'

Adam stuck his hand out, but Eric put an arm on his shoulder.

'Let's get you in the car,' he said. 'I'll give you a lift to the hospital.'

Adam stopped. 'Shouldn't we go in the ambulance?'

Eric looked at him with narrow eyes. 'You'll be fine with me.'

They got in the back of the police car, leaving the photographer to take a couple of nonchalant snaps through the window. The ambulance pulled away and they followed. Adam noticed the lifeboat untying and heading back out to sea.

'Where are they going?' he said, pointing.

Eric followed his finger. 'Back out to look for your missing friend, of course.'

'Of course.'

'They've rustled up a couple of coastguard boats to help. They're going to sweep the whole southern coastline of the Oa.'

'Reckon they'll find him?'

Eric looked carefully at Adam in the rear-view mirror. 'Better prepare yourself for the worst, son. If he's been in that water nearly twenty-four hours, the only thing they'll be finding is a corpse.'

They drove out of Port Ellen towards Bowmore. Adam remembered coming the other way less than two days ago, Roddy driving like a maniac, the world still full of possibilities. They passed the place where Joe had first pulled them over for speeding, and Adam felt sick at the sight of it.

'Didn't think you'd be working the weekend, Eric,' said Molly.

He replied over his shoulder. 'I don't normally. In fact I've almost retired these days, but there's been an emergency today.'

Adam looked at Molly, who gave him a silencing stare.

'What kind of emergency?' she said.

'I'm not meant to say,' said Eric. 'But I suppose you're connected to it.'

'Connected? In what way?' said Molly.

Adam looked at her. She sounded and looked calm. He couldn't believe it was all unravelling like this already.

'Seems they found two dead bodies first thing this morning.'

'Bodies?'

Eric nodded. 'In a burnt-out distillery.'

'One of the distilleries has burnt down?' said Molly.

'No, an illegal still. Quite a big operation, by all accounts. Just a few miles from where you were found, actually.'

'Really?'

'They haven't formally identified the bodies yet, but evidence on the scene suggests it was Joe and Grant.'

Adam could see Eric looking in the mirror for a reaction from Molly.

'Joe and Grant?' She sounded shocked and incredulous. 'In an illegal still?'

Eric nodded carefully. 'Place had burned down to the ground with them inside it.'

'Jesus,' said Molly.

Eric considered the pair of them in the back. 'Quite something. I know you and Joe were all over, but I thought you should know, given that you were man and wife for years.'

'Yeah, thanks Eric. I appreciate that. Joe and Grant, wow.'

'Anyway, I've been called in as emergency cover,' Eric said. 'Same with young Kyle who was called out to the scene of your accident. Obviously we're understaffed. But some big guns from the mainland are coming over on the ferry, to investigate the whole thing further. I was just told to get you to hospital, make sure you're OK.'

'We appreciate it, Eric, we really do,' said Molly.

'That's right,' said Adam, feeling totally redundant to the conversation, to this whole place.

They were approaching Bowmore now, swinging past the round church and down the main street, then hanging a right. The hospital was little more than a converted house with an NHS sign outside. Adam watched as the ambulance pulled up and the crew began moving Roddy inside.

Eric stopped and got out. He opened the door for Molly and helped her up.

'You've been through a lot,' he said, looking at her carefully.

'So just take it easy. They'll give you the once-over here, make sure you're OK, then I'll give you a lift back to Port Ellen.'

He turned to Adam, struggling out of the car. 'You might want to hang around, make sure your pal is OK.'

'Of course.'

'Well, let's get you inside, get you both checked out.'

Molly and Adam followed behind him, looking at each other, Adam's stomach buzzing with nerves.

37

They sat in a beige room with cheap plastic furniture waiting for a doctor to examine them. Outside the dirty window they could see Eric sitting in his police car reading a paper and smoking a pipe. Wasn't there a law against smoking in work vehicles?

'Think he suspects anything?' Adam said to Molly.

Molly looked out the window. 'Maybe, but I'm more worried about the mainland police. I don't know if anyone on Islay was working with Joe and Grant, but even if they were, they'd surely just want all this to go away after what's happened.'

'How do you mean?'

'You don't know what it's like living on an island. There's a certain mentality, a community feeling. We've always been separate from the mainland, they've ignored us for centuries, that's just the way we like it. We like to sort things out our own way.'

'I thought you didn't like it here that much?'

'I don't, but that doesn't mean I'm not part of it.'

'So if you islanders look out for each other, where does that leave me and Roddy?'

Molly frowned. 'Let's just concentrate on the mainland cops coming over on the ferry. For all we know, they could be the same guys we saw last night in the speedboat, couldn't they?'

'Shit.'

'Exactly.'

'Couldn't you organise a *Wicker Man* reception for them?' said Adam, smiling.

Molly laughed. 'I wish.'

She reached into her pocket and pulled out her phone.

'I can't believe no one missed me,' she said.

'What?'

'Twenty-four hours in hell and no one even texted to see if I was OK. No one even knew I was gone.'

Adam dug his phone out. Four bars on the signal now, battery fine, no calls or texts.

'Snap,' he said, laughing grimly. 'We really are a couple of sadsacks, aren't we?'

'Speak for yourself,' said Molly, nudging him in the ribs.

'Ow.'

The door opened and a stocky young woman wearing a white coat came in.

'Molly, you OK?' she said in a concerned voice.

'Hi, Carol,' said Molly. 'We're both doing fine, I think.'

Molly turned to Adam. 'This is Carol, Dr Mackay. Carol, this is Adam.'

'Quite something you've been through,' said Carol in a fussy voice. 'Can't believe you were out there all night. And after a crash like that. How do you feel?'

'Fine,' said Molly. 'Pretty tired, but OK.'

The doctor examined them, taking blood pressure and temperature, checking eyes, ears and throats, asking about aches and pains, checking fingers and toes. Adam stared at his hands as Carol held them, thinking about the microscopic fragments of Luke's brain probably stuck under his nails. He felt a shiver run through him, making Carol stop.

'Are you sure you're OK?'

Adam nodded. 'Just need some sleep.'

Carol nodded too. 'Terrible business about your friends. I wouldn't be surprised if you were in shock. Horrible, just horrible. Here's hoping they find the one that's still out there.'

Adam looked at Molly, who spoke. 'Eric didn't think there would be much chance of survival.'

Carol shrugged. 'You never know with these things.' She looked out the window. 'Did Eric tell you about Joe and Grant?'

Molly sighed. 'He mentioned it.'

'Shocking, really shocking,' said Carol. 'Had the bodies in here earlier, what a state. Almost nothing left of them. They haven't formally identified them, but their badges were on the scene, so they're pretty sure.'

'I see.'

Carol looked at Molly. 'I know you and Joe weren't . . . well anyway, it's still horrific.'

'Yeah.'

Carol shook her head. 'Nothing happens around here for years at a time, and now suddenly two tragic incidents within a few miles of each other on the same night. An amazing co-incidence, don't you think?'

Adam felt his jaw clench.

Molly looked Carol in the eye. 'Amazing.'

Adam butted in. 'Any news on Roddy? The guy with the shoulder injury?'

'Dr Stuart said he must've had some balls,' said Carol.

'Sitting with that in his shoulder for almost twenty-four hours.'

'Yeah,' said Adam. 'He's quite something.'

'I know Dr Stuart is taking him into surgery at the moment, I can go and find out the latest, if you like.'

'That would be great,' said Adam, giving her a feeble smile.

As she bustled out of the room, he turned to Molly.

'Reckon we can keep this up?' he said.

'What choice do we have?'

'I keep forgetting I'm supposed to be hoping they find Luke,' said Adam. 'This is a nightmare.'

They sat in silence for a while, too exhausted to speak. Adam felt his eyes begin to close, a thick wooziness sweeping over him. Confused pictures began swirling round and merging in his mind, images of the crash, Ethan face down in the rockpool, Joe grinning at them, Luke slumped on the floor, Molly bent over the cask, the chase through the geese, drowning under ice, Joe rolling around on the floor engulfed in flames, Luke's terrible missing face, the still burning in the night, the grimly comical sight of them struggling with the barrel along the coast, it all merged into a sickening whole, a dizzying mess of vivid, lurid nightmares, endlessly repeating over and over till he felt like screaming.

He snapped awake as the door opened, Carol coming back in. He looked round and saw Molly curled up asleep on the floor. He looked at the time on his phone. He'd been out for almost an hour.

'Sorry I took so long,' said Carol quietly, looking at Molly sleeping. 'You can go and see your friend now.'

'Is he OK?'

She tiptoed over to a cabinet and took out a rough woollen blanket, placing it gently over Molly.

'He's out of surgery,' she whispered. 'I don't know if he'll be conscious or not. Dr Stuart says he's an extremely fit guy, otherwise it could've been a lot worse. There's still a slim chance he could lose the arm, though. There's a big risk of septicaemia. You can't walk around with metal sticking out of your shoulder and not expect to get a serious infection.'

'But he's going to be OK, yeah?'

Carol nodded and held the door open for him. They both looked at Molly asleep on the floor, something like a smile touching the corners of her mouth. How the hell can she be happy? thought Adam. How can any of us be happy? How can any of us sleep soundly ever again?

He dragged his eyes away from her and tiptoed out of the room.

38

Even with extensive blood loss, possible poisoning and a totally fucked arm, Roddy still somehow managed to look good. He was topless, the entire right side of his chest and shoulder heavily bandaged, all the way down to his elbow. His flat stomach and rippling muscles were sickening to Adam, and while his face was pale, the skin tone on his body suggested he'd just come off the beach. Which he had, of course.

Roddy was sleeping with a peaceful look on his face. Adam stood over him, examining the faint lines bunched around his eyes. They'd been friends for twenty years. Over that time they'd both changed beyond recognition, but they'd somehow stayed in each other's orbit. How had that happened? Adam thought about how he felt when he briefly thought Roddy was dead back at the crash site. They seemed to need each other, a symbiotic relationship which didn't necessarily do either of them any good. Or did it? Adam got to feel morally superior, while Roddy got to flaunt his successful lifestyle in Adam's face. Or maybe it was the other way around – Adam got to reinforce his loser status by witnessing Roddy's success, while Roddy caught the occasional glimpse of what life could've been if he'd had a moral compass. Whatever, they certainly had something to keep them together now, this whole horrific escapade.

This struggle for survival would tether them to each other until the grave.

Roddy's eyes flickered then opened. He rolled his head to the side and looked at his bandaged arm, then turned to Adam.

'I'm gonna miss that piece of shit metal spike,' he said, grimacing through a smile.

'How are you feeling?'

'Like I've just spent twenty-four hours running around the wilderness with a bit of car in my shoulder, trying not to get killed by a maniac.'

Adam looked round at the open door, then went to close it.

'That never happened, of course,' he said.

'Of course,' said Roddy. 'What the fuck do you take me for?'

'I just wanted to make sure you were clear about our story,' said Adam. 'You were pretty out of it back there sometimes.'

'All thanks to Uncle Charlie. What happened to my case, by the way?'

Adam shook his head. 'I chucked it over the side of the lifeboat while you were out for the count. Thought it was for the best.'

'Shame, I could do with some now,' said Roddy, his body tensing as he shifted his weight.

'Here,' said Adam, lifting a button attached to a drip going into Roddy's hand. 'The nurse showed me, this is morphine. You press it to get more.'

Roddy grinned. 'Drugs on tap? That's a fucking sweet deal.'

He pressed the button and waited a few seconds. He stared at Adam, his eyes widening then narrowing. 'Oh fuck, that's good shit.' He sank into his pillows.

'So,' said Adam. 'Our story?'

'Yeah, yeah,' said Roddy dreamily. 'We crashed. Found Ethan. Luke missing. Set a fire and sat around all night till morning. Simple.'

'Cool,' said Adam. 'They've found Joe and Grant already.'

Roddy gazed glassily through the morphine. 'I knew they would. A fire that size was bound to attract attention. What're they saying?'

'We spoke to that copper Eric that Molly knows.'

'Did you tell him what really happened?'

Adam shook his head. 'Molly thought it best to just stick to our story with him too.'

'Clever girl,' said Roddy. 'She's right. Can't be too careful. The fewer people know the truth the better.'

'I don't think anyone is linking us to the fire at the still, not yet anyway. I get the impression that the other Islay cops weren't in on the bootlegging thing. Molly seems to reckon they'll just want it all to go away, so they're not looking too hard for reasons not to brush it under the carpet.'

'It can't be that easy?'

'It's not,' said Adam, shaking his head. 'Cops are coming from the mainland to look into it. Eric reckons they'll want to speak to us.'

'Right.'

'Oh, a lifeboat and a couple of coastguard boats are sweeping the coast off the Oa, searching for Luke. Remember to look hopeful that they find him.'

'They're surely not expecting to find him alive after this time?'

'No, they're searching for the body, really. Fingers crossed they don't find it for a while. Even if they do, hopefully we've done enough that forensics won't twig.'

'Depends how good a job you made of getting that bullet out.'

'I got it out fine, OK?'

'OK, only fucking saying.'

'Well don't bother,' said Adam. 'You have no idea what I went through when you were out cold back there.'

Roddy looked at his shoulder. 'I kind of had my own shit to worry about, you know.'

Adam could feel his heart racing and made a conscious effort to calm down. 'I know. Look, we just have to stay calm and stick to what we said, OK?'

'Not a problem.'

The door opened and Eric poked his head round. He looked at Roddy. 'How you doing, son?'

'Not too bad, considering.'

'That's good.' Eric looked at Adam. 'Can you follow me please, Mr Strachan? A couple of gentlemen from Strathclyde CID in Glasgow have arrived and want to have a quick word with you.' He turned back to Roddy. 'Then they want to speak with you, Mr Hunter, if you're up to it?'

'Sure,' said Roddy.

Adam patted Roddy on his good shoulder and gave him a furtive glance. Roddy smiled and pressed the button for more morphine, sinking further into his bed covers.

'That is good shit,' he said to himself as Adam headed out the door.

39

'I believe you've been through quite an ordeal.'

Adam was back in the same beige room as before, facing a tall, muscular man with a square jaw and close-cropped hair. No uniform, but he'd shown Adam his ID, Detective Inspector Ritchie. The guy looked more like a bouncer than a copper, though was there really much difference?

'Where's Molly?'

The DI gave him a look. 'Ms Gillespie is giving her version of events to my colleague.'

'Version of events?'

'Just routine,' said Ritchie. 'With any incident like this, we want to establish the chain of events, make sure we know exactly what happened.'

'But it was just a car accident.'

Ritchie smiled, no warmth in it.

'A car accident resulting in one fatality, one serious injury and one missing person, presumed dead.'

'Presumed dead?'

'You strike me as an intelligent man,' said Ritchie. 'If your friend has been in the water since the crash, he has very little chance of survival at this time of year.'

'If?'

Ritchie stared at Adam. 'Presuming you never saw him in the water, how do you know for sure that's where he ended up?'

Adam's mind raced. 'We searched all over for him after the crash, didn't find anything.'

'Maybe he woke up first, went to get help but got into trouble.'

Adam frowned. 'What kind of trouble?'

'You tell me.'

Adam looked at Ritchie. 'He wouldn't have gone off without helping us first. He would've woken us. When I came round, Molly and Roddy were still in the car, they needed to be got out. He would've done that, not just wandered off.'

'Maybe he was concussed and confused.'

'He wouldn't just wander off.'

'Or maybe he got out of the car before it went over the cliff.'

'What?' Adam could feel himself getting flustered. 'What do you mean?'

'Maybe he realised you were heading over a cliff, and somehow got out before the car went over.'

Adam shook his head. 'Then he would've gone for help, wouldn't he?'

'We just have to consider all the possibilities,' said Ritchie. The DI was absent-mindedly staring out the grimy window. 'You understand that, don't you?'

'Of course.'

Ritchie turned back. 'So, tell me what happened in your own words.'

'Doesn't there have to be two of you present for a police interview?' said Adam.

Ritchie smiled. 'I think you've been watching too much *Taggart*, Mr Strachan. This isn't a formal interview, just a little chat to establish what happened. There's no need to be so defensive.'

'I'm not being defensive,' said Adam, his blood pumping faster.

'So tell me what happened.'

'We were driving back from Stremnishmore, and . . .'

'What were you doing there?'

Adam took a moment. 'Looking at the old distillery.'

'Why?'

'What does this have to do with anything?'

'Context, Mr Strachan.'

'Fine, I had plans to renovate it, get it working again.'

'And?'

Adam stared at Ritchie. 'I was trying to persuade Roddy to invest in the idea.'

'I take it from your tone he said no.'

Adam nodded. 'We were on our way back when a sheep came out of nowhere, and Roddy swerved to avoid it. Unfortunately we were right at the edge of the cliff, and went over.'

'Mr Hunter was driving?'

'Yes.'

'Had he been drinking?'

'What?'

'It's a simple question. Had Mr Hunter been drinking?'

Adam thought back to the hipflask Roddy was glugging from as he drove.

'No,' he said.

'Are you sure?'

'Pretty sure.'

'Had he been taking any drugs?'

'What's this all about?'

Ritchie stared hard at Adam. 'A blood sample taken from Mr Hunter during surgery reveals a high level of cocaine in his system.'

Adam felt the air buzz around him. 'You'd have to take that up with Roddy.'

'I'm asking you.'

'And I'm telling you I don't know anything about it. Look, we've been through a hell of a lot here, I don't need you . . .'

Ritchie raised a placating hand. 'Settle down, Mr Strachan, I'm only asking a few questions.'

Adam could feel his pulse in his forehead, thumping away. Without realising it, he pressed the button on his broken watch. Serenity now.

'So,' said Ritchie. 'You're a whisky expert.'

'Not so much an expert,' said Adam. 'More an enthusiastic amateur.'

'And you wanted to start a distillery.'

'That was the plan.'

'Had any previous experience of distilling?'

'No.'

'Not even a little moonshine set-up at home?'

Adam realised he was rubbing at his hands, picking under his fingernails. He made a conscious effort to stop.

'That would be illegal.'

'That's a no, then?'

'That's a no.'

'Do you know anything about illegal stills?'

'Why would you ask something like that?'

Ritchie looked out the window. 'Just chatting.' He turned.

'So, back to the crash. What happened next?'

Adam rubbed his forehead. 'I woke first. I'd been thrown clear, landed further up the slope. I found Molly and Roddy in the car, got them both out. Then we went looking for the others. I found Ethan, his head was totally . . .' He stopped to take a breath. 'We took his body back to the car and waited there.'

'See, this is what I don't quite understand.'

'What?'

'You just sat there all night waiting by the car?'

'That's right.'

'You didn't think to go and get help?'

'We couldn't get back up the cliff.'

'But you could've walked round the coast. Maybe found a way up.'

'We didn't think Roddy was up to it, he was pretty badly injured. And we didn't want to just leave him.'

'So you didn't leave the scene of the accident at all?'

'Except to search for Luke in the surrounding area, no.'

'You didn't head west along the coast for a few miles.'

'I told you, no. What are you talking about?'

'I'm surprised you haven't heard from the local busybodies.'

'Heard what?'

'Your friend Ethan was not the only person to die on the Oa last night.'

'What do you mean?'

Ritchie examined Adam closely. Adam felt his stomach clench and he struggled to swallow.

'There was an incident a few miles along the coast.'

'What kind of incident?'

'Two bodies found in a burnt-out building.'

'That's terrible,' said Adam, his voice sounding flat in his own ears.

'It was an illegal still.'

Adam raised his eyebrows. 'That's what the whisky questions were about? You think I had something to do with that? Come on.'

'I didn't say that.'

'No, but you're bloody well implying it.'

Ritchie stared at him. 'So you never came across an illegal still last night.'

'I told you, we didn't leave the car.'

Ritchie looked away. 'I believe you were acquainted with the people we found in the still.'

Adam could hardly breathe. 'I doubt it, I don't really know anyone here. I've only been on the island for two days.'

'They were police officers,' said Ritchie. 'Joe McInnes and Grant Nichol. You had an altercation with them in the Ardview Inn on Friday night.'

'Those two? I wouldn't say I knew them.'

'You knew them enough to throw punches at them.'

'They attacked us, completely unprovoked.'

'You were having a drink with McInnes's wife.'

'Ex-wife,' said Adam. 'And I didn't think having a drink with someone was a bloody crime.'

'And police records have a note of Mr Hunter receiving a speeding ticket from McInnes earlier in the day.'

'I don't know what you're getting at here.'

'Why was Ms Gillespie in the car with you yesterday?'

'What?'

'I was wondering why someone you'd just met was going with you to a disused distillery.'

'I've met Molly on previous trips to Islay.'

'So you knew her when she was still McInnes's wife?'

'It's not like that,' said Adam, feeling sweat under his arms and on his palms. 'You're twisting everything round.'

'I'm just trying to work out what your relationship is with these people.'

'I don't have one.'

'And yet Ms Gillespie was in the car yesterday.'

'She just came along for the ride.' Adam could hear his voice rising, couldn't stop it. 'I'd told her my plans for the distillery, she wanted to see the place.'

'So she was just unlucky to be in the car when you crashed.'

'We were all pretty bloody unlucky, don't you think?'

Ritchie examined his fingernails calmly.

'So, back to the crash.'

'Jesus, I've told you everything.'

'You waited at the car all night.'

'That's right.'

'Setting it on fire to create a smoke signal?'

'Yeah.'

'And the fire burned all night?'

'Yeah.'

'How?'

'What?'

'How did you keep it going all night?'

'We found a canister of petrol in the boot.'

'And that was enough to keep it going all night?'

'We had to ration it, we didn't know when we would be

found, if at all.'

'Don't you think it's a bit odd that you had a smoke signal going all night, but no one saw it till morning?'

Adam shrugged. 'It's pretty remote out there. I don't suppose many folk are out and about on the Oa at night in the middle of winter.'

Ritchie gave him a sideways look. 'So you didn't see anything while you waited there.'

'Like what?'

'I don't know, you tell me.'

'I have no idea what you're talking about.'

'You didn't see any boats out at sea?'

'Boats?'

'Yes.'

Adam shook his head, thinking of the police speedboat. 'If we'd seen a boat, we would've tried to get their attention, wouldn't we?'

'So you didn't see anything out at sea the whole time you were there.'

Adam shook his head again.

'And you didn't see any smoke or flames round the coast to the west?'

'From this illegal still, you mean?'

'Precisely.'

'Nothing. We were pretty much concentrating on trying to stay warm and stay alive, you know.'

'So you don't know anything about the still?'

'We've been over this already,' Adam said, getting angry. 'If we were there, wouldn't there be some evidence of that?'

'Don't worry, a forensic team is on its way from the mainland to examine the scene.'

Adam swallowed hard, struggled to breathe. He felt incredibly hot. 'Well, if they come up with anything, which they won't, we can chat again then.'

Ritchie watched him closely. Silence buzzed around the room.

'Do you know how many suspicious deaths there have been in Islay in the last twenty years?' Ritchie said eventually.

'Of course I don't.'

'Before last night, none.'

'So what?'

'So you don't think it's a little odd?'

'What?'

'That not one single person has died in strange circumstances for twenty years in the whole of this island, then suddenly two separate incidents within five miles of each other throw up three, probably four, dead bodies?'

'There is such a thing as coincidence, you know.'

'In my line of work, coincidences almost always turn out to be connected. So I'm wondering if these two incidents are really coincidental at all.'

'I can assure you they are.'

'Can you?'

'Yes.' Adam stuck his chin out in an act of defiance he didn't really feel. 'Look, are we finished here? Any chance I can go and get some sleep? I've been through a pretty traumatic experience, you know, I don't need all this bullshit.'

'You're free to go, Mr Strachan. We have your details. Please don't leave the island until we've finished our inquiries.'

'I have got a life to get back to, you know.'

Ritchie glanced at him. 'But of course you'll want to stay until the coastguard have finished their search for your friend?'

Adam blinked, his eyelids heavy as slabs. 'Of course.'

'We'll be in touch again soon, once forensics have taken a look at the two sites.'

'You do that,' said Adam, heading out the door as calmly as he could. He felt his legs shake beneath him and hoped he would get out of sight before they gave way.

40

Adam drifted in and out of a fitful sleep in the back of the police car, harrowing images gnawing at his mind. He jerked awake as they bumped over a pothole, his eyes focusing on the officer at the wheel. It was the kid who'd been called out by the old woman to the crash site earlier today. Adam could see nasty boils lining the back of his neck at his collar line, and felt the urge to reach forward and squeeze.

He looked out the window. The same flat expanse of heather, bracken and moor stretching for miles, yet somehow it all seemed so different from the first time they'd driven along here, stopped by Joe for speeding. Back then it had been a land waiting to be discovered, an adventure waiting to happen. Now it was just the backdrop for a nightmare that would forever be playing in his head.

The snow from yesterday had all but melted, tiny pockets of ice and slush lurking in the shadowed crevices of the land. He was suddenly sick of this place, sick to death of the wide open spaces and the never-ending skies and the stench of peat everywhere.

They drove past the airport then past thousands of geese hunkered against a driving wind. He remembered last night and the geese on the frozen loch, everything drenched in eerie purple light from Joe's flare, a cacophony of noise as the birds filled the black sky.

He wondered about forensic evidence, about tracks in the snow, discarded flares, the hole in the ice, the farmhouse they'd broken into. Shit, he was still wearing someone else's clothes, for Christ's sake. His heart tripped over itself as it dawned on him. Fuck, his clothes. His clothes were still sitting in a wet pile in the hallway of that farmhouse. Why the hell hadn't he thought of it before? All that worry about forensic evidence at the still and the car crash, what about the farmhouse?

He tried to get his fatigue-drenched mind to work. There was nothing to identify him amongst that stuff, nothing obvious like a wallet or phone, but it was surely covered in his DNA. What if the break-in had already been reported, his clothes already handed in to the police, the farmhouse added to the list of places to be forensically examined?

He tried to calm down. The house didn't seem to be occupied for the winter, it might be months before his clothes were discovered. Maybe there was plenty of time for him or Molly or someone else to go round and sort it. Or maybe the mainland forensic team had already searched the area and found it all. Did they have a reason to go that far from the still? He looked out again at the melted snow. Maybe their tracks had disappeared with the rising sun, then again maybe they hadn't.

Jesus, he couldn't stand to think about any of this bullshit any more. But he couldn't stop either. He churned it all round in his mind, trying to gain some clarity, trying to make sense of the mess of the situation, the mess of their lives, but his brain was mush. Maybe he was in shock. The fact he even thought of that was probably an indication that he wasn't in shock at all, just hopelessly confused and stressed.

They descended into Port Ellen then crept along the main crescent by the bay. Adam glanced at the Ardview as they passed, a couple of hardy smokers trying to shelter in the doorway from the wind. No sign of Ash.

The policeman dropped him at his B&B without a word, then did a U-turn and drove off. He watched the car disappear round the corner, then stood for a long time looking at the sea, ruffled in the wind, the occasional gull taking a dive-bombing chance into the surf, coming up with nothing. He looked at the B&B, same as every other house on the street. He noticed the nameplate, something in Gaelic that he'd never said out loud, didn't know how to pronounce. He walked through the front door, dreading seeing the old woman who ran the place. He couldn't think about having to explain everything to her. He knew she would probably already know, thanks to the island jungle drums, but that didn't make it any easier. She might be listening out for him, anxious to get the gory details first hand.

He crept up the stairs and opened the door to his room. He stopped. He'd been sharing the room with Ethan, Luke sleeping next door with Roddy. He looked at all Ethan's stuff – the Samsonite case, his dress shoes, his jumper, T-shirts and underwear neatly folded on a shelf, a plain navy-blue shirt hanging in the wardrobe, his toilet bag on the small dresser. He walked over and lifted a sleeve of the shirt, sniffed it. Smelt of Ethan, whatever deodorant he used. Fucking hell. He walked over to the dresser and sat looking in the mirror at his saggy, hangdog face. This was terrible, the remains of a life, all neatly sitting here, waiting for Ethan to come back. But he would never come back.

A bottle of Laphroaig quarter cask that Ethan had bought

from the distillery gift shop sat unopened in a bag. Adam thought back to that tour, Roddy winding him up about Molly's lack of a wedding ring.

He fetched a glass from the en suite, broke the seal on the bottle and glugged the glass half full. He held it up and pointed it at the hanging shirt.

'Here's to you, Ethan.'

It felt empty, a completely hollow gesture. He was just drinking another man's whisky, a dead man's whisky, without permission, that was all. He tried to imbue each sip with something, some kind of feeling, but nothing came.

He calmly downed the remains of the dram, then stood up and hurled the glass at the wardrobe. He watched as it smashed, sending chunks and shards scattering across the room. He sat back down with his head in his hands for a long time. When he looked up he realised he couldn't stand to be here a moment longer.

He crunched across broken glass then sneaked down the stairs and out the front door, feeling the blast of sea air on his face. He stood there wavering for a moment, then walked along the road to Molly's house.

He stood looking at the doorbell. Nothing about the house had changed since the last time he was here. Why should it have? Everything in his life was different, everything had been turned on its head, but here were bricks and mortar, implacable and unaffected by it all.

He was about to ring the bell when the door opened and Ash came stumbling out, pulling her jacket on. She walked right into him and jumped.

'Fuck, you gave me a fright,' she said.

She looked the same – hungover and strung out, sad and lost, bags under her eyes bigger than ever.

'Heard you had quite an adventure,' she said, eyeing him suspiciously.

How much had Molly told her?

'Yeah.'

'I didn't even realise Molly was missing,' she said, a tinge of guilt in her voice.

'Well, we weren't gone that long.'

It seemed insane to be talking about what they'd been through in such a matter-of-fact way. Presumably Molly hadn't told her anything about what really happened, sticking to the crash story.

Ash looked at her watch. 'If I wasn't already half an hour late for my shift, I'd kick your sorry arse for getting my sister mixed up in a stupid fucking car crash in the middle of nowhere.'

'Fair enough.'

'So count yourself lucky.'

'Believe me, I do.'

She had her jacket on now and was past him, talking over her shoulder. 'She's inside, on you go,' she said. 'But don't get her into any more shit, OK?'

'OK.'

She was halfway down the street, walking backwards and shouting. 'I mean it. Or I'll fucking kill you.'

41

Adam headed into the hall. He heard a television on and walked towards the living room. Molly was sitting on the sofa with a blanket over her, the same one Adam had found draped over himself when he woke on that sofa yesterday morning. She was staring glassy-eyed out the window, a huge tumbler of amber liquid in her hand. A black-and-white film was on television, a posh-looking couple running across moorland, just like the stuff outside.

Molly turned her head to look at the whisky bottle on the coffee table. 'Help yourself,' she said, taking a large gulp from her tumbler. 'Use Ash's glass.' She pointed at an empty glass, sticky residue lining the inside of it.

Adam walked over and picked up the bottle. It had a plain white label on it, *Port Ellen*. He'd never seen it before, it didn't have the usual age or percentage information. He poured a large measure and nosed it out of habit, but he didn't need an amazing whisky now, he needed an anaesthetic or a sleeping pill, something to erase the last thirty-six hours.

'What is it?' he said, lifting his glass.

Molly stared out the window. 'Thirty-year-old, bottled in '84. Completely unofficial. Never left the island, not for sale. Fell off the back of a lorry. It was part of my dad's special stash.'

Adam had another big sip. He didn't know what to say.

Molly seemed in a trance. He stared at her. She looked exhausted and traumatised, but still pretty, her face still strong. An image of her bent over the barrel in the still with her jeans down flashed through his mind, the look on her face back then. He gripped his glass and screwed his eyes shut, then opened them again. He looked at the old film on the television. The couple were booking into an inn and looking suspicious.

Everything was ruined now, he realised.

'I can't sleep,' said Molly, still looking out the window. 'Isn't that weird? Apart from crashing out for an hour at hospital, we've been awake for two days, walked and run for umpteen miles, been through hell, and still I can't sleep.'

'I'm the same,' said Adam, feeling enormously tired all of a sudden, as if his legs would buckle. He eased himself down into a chair facing the sofa and stared at Molly. They couldn't go back now, was all he kept thinking, they couldn't ever go back. Why did it all have to happen to them?

'How was your police interview?' asked Molly.

'A nightmare.'

She finally turned to look at him. 'You stuck to the story though, yeah?'

'Of course. But I think he knew we'd been there.'

'Same with me. But they don't know anything, not unless we tell them. They only suspect.'

They both drank, then Adam spoke.

'They said forensics were on their way.'

'Yeah.'

'What do you think they'll find?'

'No idea,' said Molly, her eyes seeming to clear. 'The still was presumably pretty much demolished in the fire.'

'What about our tracks around it? And up at the loch?'

Molly shook her head. 'I just don't know.'

'How far do you think they'll look?'

Molly didn't speak, just shrugged.

Adam swallowed uncomfortably. 'My clothes are lying on the floor in that farmhouse.'

Molly looked at him then pressed her fingers at her temples and scrunched her eyes shut. 'Oh, Jesus.'

'I know. What should we do?'

'Is there anything identifying you?'

Adam shook his head. 'Remember, Joe made us empty our pockets, so I had nothing on me. My DNA will be all over the clothes, though.'

Molly sat thinking for a moment, the corners of her mouth turned down. 'We just have to hope forensics don't get as far as the farmhouse, and that no one reports the break in for a while.'

'Is that it?'

'We can't do anything about it just now, the whole area will be crawling with police.'

'Yeah, I know, but . . .'

'It didn't look as if anyone was living there for the winter. With any luck the break-in won't be discovered till spring. In a few days, once this has all died down, I'll go out there and get your clothes.'

'Really?'

Molly looked away. 'Sure.'

They sat in silence for a while.

'Think they'll find Luke?' Adam said eventually.

'Hopefully not for a while.'

'So we just have to sit tight.'

'Looks like it.'

They both drank again.

'It's unbearable,' said Adam.

'I know,' said Molly, draining her glass and holding it out empty. 'But we just have to bear it, don't we?'

Adam struggled out of his chair, refilled both their glasses then slumped back down. He gazed at Molly. She'd hardly made eye contact since he'd come in. It broke his heart.

'How are you?' he asked.

'OK.'

'I mean after . . .'

'I know what you mean.'

'At least you got your revenge.'

Molly glared at him, locking eyes for the first time. 'You think that helps?'

'No, of course not, I didn't mean . . .'

'It's not a matter of revenge.'

'I know, I know, I'm sorry. I didn't mean it like that.'

'Then what did you mean?'

'I don't know.' He felt tears well up in his eyes. 'Jesus, I'm sorry, I just . . .'

He could feel Molly looking at him as he started to cry, his eyes stinging with tears, his breath halting. After a while he recovered himself, wiped his eyes with his sleeves, took a hit of whisky.

'Sorry,' he said.

'Don't be,' said Molly. 'I'm sorry. I shouldn't take it out

on you.'

There was a long silence, just the low chatter of the couple on television, who were now in a bedroom, handcuffed together.

'So what now?' Adam said after a while.

Molly sipped and shrugged. 'I've got work tomorrow.'

'You're not seriously thinking of going in, are you?'

'What else am I going to do?'

'Surely they'd understand you're in no fit state.'

'I don't mind,' said Molly. 'Better than sitting around here.'

Molly looked at him, and he spotted a glimmer of the kindness in her eyes that he'd first noticed, the affection she had for him before all this insanity.

'What about you?' she said.

'I'm supposed to stay on the island until the police get back in touch. Roddy presumably won't be out of hospital for a while. Then there's Ethan.'

He fell silent. Was he supposed to deal with Ethan's body? Shit, what about Debs, he hadn't even called her. Was that his responsibility? He couldn't face speaking to her. It would've been bad enough with a simple crash, but everything else, all the secrets and stupid lies they had to maintain, it was all just impossible. Everything was completely fucked up. How were they supposed to survive all this shit?

He felt a wave of immense fatigue sweep over him. He downed his whisky and rubbed at his face. He was stinking, he hadn't showered in days. He noticed Molly was scrubbed clean, her hair still slightly damp.

'Think I need to have a wash, get some rest maybe,' he said, creaking out of the chair.

'OK,' said Molly, looking up at him.

Adam looked her in the eye. 'Can I come back later?'

Molly held his gaze for a moment then looked away. 'I don't think so.'

'I don't want to be alone.'

'I don't think it'll do any good for us to see each other.'

'What do you mean?'

Adam stared at her, his heart thumping. Serenity now.

Molly looked at him and he struggled to swallow.

'I don't think we should keep in touch.'

'What, ever?'

Molly finished her drink and put her glass down. 'We'll just remind each other of it all.'

Adam gulped heavily. 'So what?'

She looked at him. 'I don't want to be reminded of it. Any of it.'

'But . . .' Adam realised he didn't have an answer. He couldn't bear it. It was all so fucking fucked up. 'So this is it?'

Molly looked at him kindly. 'Sorry, Adam, I just think it's for the best.'

'But I want to see you again.'

Molly smiled thinly. 'Maybe you will, if there's a court case.'

'God, don't say that.'

Molly rubbed her chin. 'Let's just try and forget any of this ever happened, OK?'

Adam knew that was impossible, and he knew Molly knew it too. He looked her in the eyes for a long time until eventually she turned away to watch the television.

He kept staring at her in silence, not knowing what to do or say. Eventually he just sighed and turned to leave, his body exhausted beyond words and his mind buzzing with miserable nightmares.

42

A police car was parked outside the B&B.

Adam felt the malt coursing through his veins. He'd had three huge drams in the last hour and felt dizzy, his tongue dry and rough, a drouth coming on. He stopped a hundred yards from the car and tried to think. What did it mean? Had forensics found something already? Had the coastguard found Luke? Were they taking him back in for more questioning? He didn't think he could cope with that.

Maybe he should disappear. There was plenty of space on this God forsaken island, he could merge into the landscape, live off the land for a while. He laughed at his own stupidity. He'd almost died after a single day in the wilderness. He hadn't eaten since breakfast yesterday. And yet he had no appetite, just rocks in his stomach, stones of worry rubbing away at his innards, eroding him from the inside out.

He could make out someone sitting in the car waiting for him. It didn't look like the mainland inspector, the intimidating bouncer guy. Maybe this wouldn't be so bad after all. He had to face it sooner or later anyway, he had nowhere else to go.

Molly didn't want him at her place, didn't want to see him ever again. Part of him could understand that. He wasn't being punished, it wasn't his fault, his presence in her life would be too much of a reminder. But that didn't mean he wasn't upset about it. They'd been through so much together, he felt a part of her life now in a visceral way he couldn't have imagined, and the thought of never seeing her again made his heart pound and his body shake. Or maybe that was the whisky and the exhaustion and the shock finally kicking in.

He righted himself and walked towards the car, trying to keep his legs going straight and his chin raised.

As he approached, the driver's door opened and a figure got out. It was Eric. Adam attempted a smile, and Eric smiled back as he came round the car to meet him.

'Something up?' said Adam, trying to sound upbeat.

Eric's smile faded.

'Pack your things,' he said nonchalantly. 'And all your friends' stuff too. You're getting the next ferry back to the mainland.'

Adam was confused. 'But that Ritchie guy said I had to stay on the island until he got in touch again.'

'Never mind what he said. I'm all the law you need to worry about on Islay at the moment, and I'm telling you to pack up. You're leaving.'

'What's this about?'

'I'll explain in the car,' said Eric. 'We don't have much time, the ferry will be getting into Port Askaig soon.'

Adam stood there, swaying a little.

Eric put a hand on his shoulder. 'If you don't want your belongings, you can leave without them. Either way, you're getting on that boat.'

'I don't understand,' said Adam.

'You don't have to.' Eric was starting to sound annoyed. 'I said I would explain in the car.'

Eric gave him a gentle shove towards the B&B and Adam started walking, frowning over his shoulder.

Eric called after him. 'And don't worry about paying your bill, it's been settled.'

Adam headed up the stairs and into his room, his nose filling with the antiseptic stench of spilled whisky, his feet grinding glass shards into the thin carpet. He quickly threw all his stuff into his bag, then chucked all Ethan's neatly stacked clothes into his suitcase. He stopped to glug some quarter cask from the bottle, throwing it into his bag. He had a quick check round the room, then went through to Roddy and Luke's room.

He couldn't work out what this was all about. Could he trust this Eric guy? Molly had said he was a good sort, but what did that mean? She'd also decided not to tell him the truth, so maybe he couldn't be trusted after all. Or maybe she had told him. He certainly seemed a better bet than that Ritchie character, but that wasn't saying much. Fuck it, he was too exhausted and too wasted to work out what the hell was going on. It was easier just to go with the flow and take what came his way.

He threw Roddy and Luke's stuff into their bags. He felt ill as he saw Luke's belongings and thought about the gaping head wound, the bullet, the feel of raw flesh and bone against his fingers. He wondered where Luke was now, whether he'd already washed up somewhere along the coast, or if he was bobbing miles out to sea, maybe heading all the way over the ocean to another continent. He wondered about the fish and birds that would peck and nibble at him, the terrible storms that would blow him about, helpless and cold in that vast expanse. He ran to the toilet and puked up single malt all over the bowl and the floor. Didn't matter, Eric said the bill was already paid. He rinsed his mouth from the tap then lugged the two bags out the door.

He went back into his room. He got his bag and Ethan's case, then carried all four of them down the stairs, banging off the banister and struggling under the weight, his legs unsteady. The landlady was nowhere to be seen. Where was she?

Outside Eric took the bags from him and threw them in the back, then opened the passenger door. Adam looked at him.

'Just get in,' said Eric, looking at his watch.

Adam looked at his own watch, broken since the crash, and wondered what time it was, what he was doing, how this was all going to end.

He got into the police car then reached in the back, opened his bag and took out Ethan's Laphroaig. He unplugged it and took a swig. He could hardly taste anything, his throat raw from vomiting, just a massive hit of peat overwhelming his senses, a taste so familiar yet now somehow completely alien, as if he'd never tasted single malt whisky before in his life.

He pulled his seat belt on as Eric got in.

'That quarter cask?' said Eric, eyeing the bottle.

Adam nodded.

'Mind if I have a wee dram?'

Adam handed it over. 'Help yourself.'

Eric uncorked it, wiped the rim and took a big swig, smacking his lips theatrically. He took another drink then recorked it and handed it back.

'That's a fine malt,' he said, putting his seat belt on.

Adam felt numb. 'Yeah.'

Eric started the engine and pulled away. They were heading for the ferry. As they climbed out of Port Ellen, Eric turned to Adam.

'We know you were there,' he said.

43

Adam looked at Eric driving. He had a kind face, weather-beaten but full of compassion, his thick grey hair swept back and his chunky hands firm on the steering wheel. He looked like he'd be a fantastic grandad to some little sprogs.

Adam turned to look out the window. They were driving back up the same stupid road he was sick of, stretches of ugly brown shrubs cowering in a sharp, squally wind that spattered the windscreen with dirty rain. The wipers scraped across with a nerve-shredding rhythm, struggling to keep the windscreen clean.

They were doing eighty easily, Adam feeling every bump and pothole judder through his bones thanks to the shit suspension. The heating was up full and he was suffocating, struggling to breathe. He glugged at the malt, but that only warmed him further, made his insides itchy.

'What?' he said finally.

'I said we know you were there.'

Adam stared at him for a long time then looked out the window at the gloom. 'I don't know what you're talking about.'

Eric smiled. 'Of course you do.'

'I really don't.'

Eric glanced at Adam. 'Want me to spell it out?'

Adam shrugged. 'Sounds like you're dying to, so knock

yourself out.'

'Is that yes or no?'

Adam laughed despite himself. He looked at Eric. 'That's a yes.'

Eric kept his eyes on the road.

'We know you were at the still last night . . .'

'I already told Ritchie that's bullshit.'

Eric held up a placating hand. 'It doesn't matter what you told DI Ritchie. I'm not Ritchie. Do you want to hear what I've got to say or not?'

Adam waved his hand in a vague gesture of acquiescence.

'We know you were at the still last night. You met Joe and Grant there. We know that one of you got injured or killed, probably shot or stabbed. I presume that was your friend Luke, the one the coastguard are still looking for. We know there was some kind of chase up to Loch Kinnabus and someone went through the ice. Also, you broke into the farmhouse at Upper Killeyan where whoever went through the ice changed out of their freezing wet clothes.' Eric eyed Adam's baggy jumper and fleece. 'Then you walked back along the cliffs to the barn. We know you had something to do with the fire, and that you then trekked back to the car. It seems you were pushing a barrel, presumably with Luke's body inside. You must've thrown him in the sea at some point, I'm guessing because of the evidence of his wounds.'

Adam felt himself gulp heavily. He turned to face Eric.

'That is one hell of an imagination you've got there.'

Eric laughed. 'You think so? Actually, I'm pretty sure my imagination couldn't come up with anything so outlandish.'

This was it, they were all going to jail for a long time. Adam felt strangely untouched by the thought, as if the whole matter concerned someone else.

'So where are you getting all this shit from?' he said.

Eric smiled again. 'Your tracks were all over the place. When we got to the still this morning there were tracks in the snow leading off the path west to Loch Kinnabus, as well as east along the coast, back towards the Audi. There were markings from barrel staves and hoops in that direction as well. It didn't take a brain surgeon to work out what had happened once we got the call from Mrs Leary about your car crash.'

Adam flinched at the phrase 'brain surgeon' and saw his hands in the mess of Luke's head. He picked at his nails, then the skelf still lodged in his finger.

'We were never there,' Adam deadpanned. 'We had nothing to do with it.'

Eric took his eyes off the road and examined Adam. Adam saw a world-weary look in the old-timer's eyes.

Eric put a big hand on Adam's arm.

'It's OK, son,' he said. 'We've fixed it.'

Adam frowned. He drank from the Laphroaig bottle to give his hands something to do, but the bottle shook and he dribbled down his chin. He wiped himself, staring forwards, not wanting to look at Eric's face.

'What do you mean?'

Eric returned his hand to the wheel and his eyes to the road.

'It's amazing how much damage to forensic evidence you can do with a fire engine, three squad cars and umpteen willing pairs of feet,' he said. 'Especially when you're mostly talking about tracks in the snow which were melting anyway.

Plus water damage from the fire engine's hose is all over the place. All that coming and going with vehicles and officers on foot, it just made a complete mess of the whole area, so much so that there's probably no evidence left in the immediate vicinity that you were ever there. And nothing leading to the tracks further afield.'

'We weren't ever there,' said Adam warily.

'Of course not,' said Eric.

They drove in silence for a bit, Adam sipping whisky, the wipers scraping at the windscreen, hot air swirling around them.

'OK,' said Adam eventually. 'Suppose for a second that there was evidence we were there. I'm not admitting we were, of course. But just suppose.'

'Just suppose,' said Eric.

'Why the hell would you destroy it?'

Eric sighed. 'You know nothing about the Ileach, do you?'

'This is some stupid island thing?'

'Nothing stupid about it. I knew Molly's mother and father well, they were friends of mine. It was really hard for her and Ashley when they passed away, and Molly has done her best ever since to look after her little sister.' Eric glanced at Adam. 'We look after our own here on Islay.'

'Molly said something similar.'

'When we heard that Molly was part of the crash, we knew she must've been at the still as well. We didn't want her mixed up in any of that. Luckily we were in a position to do something about it.'

'Who's "we"?'

'The Islay police.'

'But Joe and Grant were Islay police.'

Eric puffed out his cheeks. 'Joe and Grant didn't exactly have many friends. They bullied their way through life, treated everyone with disrespect and often much worse. Like Molly, for example. Frankly, Islay is a better place now that they're dead.'

Something occurred to Adam. 'Did you know what they were up to on the Oa?'

Eric nodded. 'We didn't like it, but there didn't seem much we could do about it.'

'You could've tried to shut them down.'

Eric shrugged. 'They were strong-minded boys, I don't think they would've taken that too well. It's over now anyway.'

'Who were they working with? There were other police involved, collecting deliveries.'

Eric turned to him. 'How would you know that if you were never at the still?'

Adam felt a rush of blood to his cheeks.

Eric smiled. 'It's OK, son.' He slowed the car for a bend, then back up through the gears. 'There were a few mainland officers involved, that's correct.'

'Is Ritchie one of them?'

'I don't think so,' said Eric. 'We're pretty sure it was a small operation, it didn't go too far up. I get the impression that DI Ritchie is as shocked and dismayed by the whole thing as his superiors will be when they find out, something else which could work in your favour.'

'How do you mean?'

'I suspect those higher up will be doing everything in their power to have this whole thing brushed under the carpet. It doesn't exactly reflect well on the reputation of Strathclyde Police that two of their officers were running an illegal whisky operation, and died suspiciously in the process. I don't think they need the added complication of members of the public being involved.'

Adam took a big swig of quarter cask and made a decision. 'Grant was an accident. But with Joe . . .'

Eric frowned. 'Don't say anything else.'

'But I want to tell you what happened.'

'It doesn't matter what happened and it's better I don't know.'

'Doesn't it matter?'

'Not to me. All that matters is that Molly is home safe and that you and your friend are off the island by the end of the day.'

'Roddy's leaving too? I thought he'd be in hospital for days.'

'He discharged himself on the strong recommendation of a colleague of mine. They're meeting us at Port Askaig.'

'But Ritchie told us to stay.'

'Let us worry about DI Ritchie,' said Eric. 'We'll just say we got our wires crossed, breakdown in communication, something like that. He thinks we're all incompetent hicks anyway, after the mess we made of the crime scene.'

Adam stared out the window. It was getting dark fast, the gloom encroaching all around, so that all he could see was his own dim reflection on the glass and the occasional lonely house lit up on the moors outside. Islay looked like anywhere else in the world, just another rural backwater trying to survive.

'I've got something for you,' said Eric.

He reached behind Adam's seat, produced a carrier bag and plonked it on Adam's lap. Adam opened it tentatively and saw his clothes inside, the ones he'd left at the farmhouse.

They were neatly folded. He touched the jacket on the top. It was dry and still faintly warm. He felt a rush of raw emotion and his eyes began to sting. He fought back tears, then turned to Eric.

'You seem to have everything covered.'

'Not quite.' Eric slowed the car as they descended towards Port Askaig. 'Ritchie will be in touch with you back in Edinburgh. We can't do anything about that. No matter what he says, just stick to your story.'

'Of course.'

'One other thing,' said Eric as they snaked down the road cut in the cliff face, the lights of the Port Askaig Hotel shimmering below. 'If the coastguard find your friend's body and it's not too sea-damaged, will it tie you to Joe and Grant?'

Adam felt a shiver as he glugged more malt. He looked at the bottle. It was half empty already. 'I don't think so.'

'Good,' said Eric as they pulled up behind a parked police car. 'Now let's get you the hell off Islay.'

44

The rain had stopped and it was dark now. Adam got out and felt a wet wind on his face, blowing in from the Sound of Islay, carrying a decaying fishy smell mixed with diesel and seaweed. It reminded him of a ropy eight-year-old Caol Ila he'd had once in a pub in Leith. Caol Ila was about two miles up the coast. It had been on his itinerary for a visit this weekend, something that made him grimace and laugh sadly to himself. If only they'd stuck to visiting distilleries instead of his idiotic plan to open one, maybe there would be four of them about to get on the ferry out of here instead of just two.

The back door of the other police car opened and Adam could hear Roddy swearing at the driver, who didn't speak or move. Roddy struggled to get out of the car, moaning in pain and muttering under his breath.

'Don't just fucking stand there,' he said when he spotted Adam. 'Help me the fuck out of this car, will you?'

Adam offered an arm of support as Roddy eased onto his feet. In the jaundiced glow of the streetlights he looked like an evil ghost, ashen-faced, large bags under his eyes, sweat prickling his brow even in the cold wind. Adam wondered how he looked to Roddy.

'Some fucking chauffeur service, eh?' said Roddy, glancing at the policeman in the car. 'Can't even help a seriously injured and completely innocent man out of his car.'

'Give it a rest,' said Adam.

Roddy grinned and slapped Adam on the back. 'Well, it looks like we're getting off this God-forsaken dump of an island after all, doesn't it? Any idea what the hell is going on? I couldn't get anything out of Igor here.' Roddy pointed a thumb at his driver, still sitting implacable.

'Yeah, I have a fair idea,' said Adam, watching Eric get out of his squad car and come round to join them. 'I'll tell you later.'

Roddy turned to Eric. 'I was having a great time in that hospital, you know. Morphine on tap; a couple of cute nurses to flirt with. Then your mate here comes along and forces me out of bed, just when I was getting comfy. Any chance of an explanation?'

Eric looked at Adam then Roddy, shook his head. 'Your friend has just said he'll fill you in later. Meantime, you boys have a ferry to catch.'

He looked beyond them, making Adam and Roddy turn. The large ship was lit up, sparkling its way in to dock at the jetty, churning up wake as its engines chugged loudly into reverse to slow its progress, swinging round expertly till its prow was perfectly aligned with the apron ramp.

The sight of it dominating the tiny port held them mesmerised for a moment, watching its elegant manoeuvres, a strange mix of swan-like grace and brutal engineering.

The bow door descended and they heard car and lorry engines coughing into life, then a steady stream of vehicles slid out and up the steep slope away from Port Askaig, headlights sweeping round the rocks and trees then away, plunging the surrounding land back into darkness.

A handful of punters came out of the adjacent hotel and

280

got into their cars, starting engines in the queue then slowly crawling into the ferry's open mouth. Adam tried to think of their journey over here on the same boat only two and a half days ago, but it seemed so faint in his mind, like a dream, a vision of a simpler, quieter life before everything had become broken.

He turned to see Eric dump their bags on the pavement next to him. Four bags, two passengers. Adam gazed at Ethan and Luke's bags, then at the Laphroaig bottle in his hand. He uncorked it and took several gulps.

'Hey, don't hog that,' said Roddy. 'I could use a wee dram right now.'

Adam passed the bottle over and looked at Eric.

'A word of advice,' said Eric, looking at them both. 'Never, ever set foot on Islay again, all right?'

'Don't worry,' said Roddy. 'After this weekend, it's right at the bottom of my holiday destination list.'

'I mean it,' Eric said to Adam. 'I don't expect a sensible reply from this idiot . . .'

'Hey,' said Roddy.

'. . . but you seem a decent sort. So please, just do as I say and never come back. It's best for everyone if you stay away.'

Adam nodded as he took the bottle back from Roddy and drank.

'We will.'

Eric looked at the bottle. Adam was holding it lazily by the neck, only a quarter full now. In his other hand, the carrier bag full of his clothes hung limply.

'And maybe you should lay off the malt for a while,' said Eric kindly.

Adam gave a little snort of laughter and put the cork back in the bottle. He slung it and the carrier bag into his holdall then picked it up, along with Ethan's case and Luke's bag. Eric handed the fourth bag to Roddy.

'Goodbye, lads,' he said. 'Safe home now.'

Adam and Roddy turned and headed towards the ferry. Adam tried to let the engine roar and diesel stench fill his mind, blank out the images of Luke and Ethan.

45

Adam stared at the retreating lights of the Port Askaig Hotel, the fiercely bitter wind dragging tears from his eyes. Soon they rounded a bend in the Sound of Islay and the island lights were lost, just the huge, hulking mass of moors and cliffs and peat bogs alongside, shadowy and looming in the dark.

His hands were freezing, clutching Ethan's quarter-cask bottle to his chest. He fumbled to uncork it then took two large hits, only just feeling the burn in his chest through the numbness of his mind and body. He looked at the bottle as he shoved the cork back in. It was almost finished.

He was on his own. Roddy had nipped inside to change out of his blood-soaked clothes, which were drawing attention and comment from other passengers. How had they ever become friends? How had they stayed friends over the years, with nothing whatsoever in common? He tried to think back to moments before the crash, Roddy driving like a maniac, drinking and snorting, angry at being dragged out to Stremnishmore and asked for money. Adam saw his own arm swinging through the air towards Roddy's head, catching him on the ear, Roddy turning in anger. Then there was just darkness, so much evil in the darkness, so much to be scared of, so much to run away from.

And here he was running again. Running away from Islay and Molly, leaving her to cope on her own. Not that he thought for a minute she couldn't cope on her own. But he wanted to be there, wanted to be part of her life, wanted to have the time to get to know her, to fall in love with her and live happy ever after.

What a joke. There was no happy ever after, not after everything that had happened. Molly would be fine, in fact she might even do a lot better on the island with Joe out of the picture. She would go on living her life, doing what she had to to survive, all the while keeping the dark secrets of the weekend tight within her chest like a tumour, a small malignant lump of anger and sorrow within her.

He would never see her again. He tried to get his head round that. He closed his eyes and tried to picture her at the Laphroaig distillery, wearing that green uniform, eyes sparkling, friendly smile. But he couldn't. All he could picture was her bent over the barrel, blank terror in her eyes, or sitting staring out the window of her living room, dram in hand, an exhausted and empty look on her face.

An image of Joe tore into his brain, the stench of his burning flesh, the sight of his melting face, bubbling and blistering as he frantically waved his arms about. Adam hoped he wouldn't lose any sleep over that, but he was afraid he might.

The same went for Ethan and Luke. So many ghosts, so much lost. So much carnage, pointless carnage, all because of a stupid car crash and an unlucky stumble into a crazy world.

He thought about Luke's body, still out there in the freezing cold sea, blue and bloated now, tossed around by waves and tides like flotsam. He looked at Ethan's Laphroaig bottle in his hands. There were about two swigs left in the bottom of the bottle. He uncorked it, carefully sipped, then slid the cork back in firmly and examined it. Just enough left in there for a decent

dram. He made sure the cork was in tight then leaned back and
hurled the bottle as hard as he could high into the blustery air.
It flew into the night, spiralling neck over tail and falling into
the surrounding blackness before finally hitting the water.

The wind roaring in his ears and the heavy thrum of the ferry
engines drowned out any splash. He could just make out the
bottle bobbing in the rough seas, appearing and disappearing
from view, then finally gone into the dark.

'That's to see you on your way, Luke,' he shouted into the
wind, the words whipped into nothingness immediately.

He wondered where the bottle would end up. Maybe the
currents would take it on an adventure around the world.
Maybe the waves would do the same for Luke, take him on
the trip of a lifetime, take him to witness things he could
never have dreamed of. He hoped Ethan's bottle would find
him, give him a send-off into whatever adventure the ocean
saw fit to give him.

He remembered something and knelt to open his holdall. He
took out his jacket, went through the pockets and pulled out a
wad of congealed paper mulch. It was his distillery plans, soaked
in the loch and then dried along with his clothes, utterly useless now, just a shapeless lump of indecipherable pulp. He tried
to prise a few sheets apart, but bits just flaked off in his hands,
crumbling to pieces that were whipped away by the wind. He
leant over the railing and opened his fingers, releasing the paper
wad so that it tumbled down into the dark. He watched as it
quickly dissolved and was scattered by the relentless waves.

He thought about his own body following, tipping over the
small handrail and into the inky, oily mass of the sea. What
would it feel like to throw yourself into the water? The sudden

shock of the cold knocking the breath from your lungs, the icy fingers of water surrounding you, dragging you under into blissful oblivion, wiping all the evil thoughts from your mind, erasing your whole being, absorbing you into its unfathomable vastness, its cold, unthinking expanses.

His hands gripped the rail tightly, his fingers numb. He could easily imagine his body moving quickly up and over, then falling freely down into the deep. Then it seemed like he was really doing it, felt like he was climbing up onto the handrail, his blank mind watching it all from afar. He couldn't work out how his body was moving, but it was, he was being drawn inexorably towards the churning wash beneath the ferry, hypnotised by the endless ebb and flow of the water below, calling him downwards, pleading for him to join with it.

46

He felt a strong tug on his arm and fell back from the edge.

'What the fuck are you playing at?' Roddy shouted, holding on to his sleeve. 'You could've fallen in.'

'Maybe that's the point.'

Roddy rolled his eyes. 'Oh please, fucking spare me. I'm not going to have to spend this whole trip on suicide watch, am I? Come on, you're better than this.'

'Am I?'

'Yeah, you fucking well are.'

'I'm not so sure.'

Roddy shook his head. 'I'm not going to give you the whole "You've got so much to live for" bullshit, you know all that.'

'Don't you feel anything?'

'About what?'

'About everything that's happened. About Ethan and Luke.'

'Of course I do,' said Roddy. 'I'm not a complete fucking moron. I know you think I am, but I'm not. I've been through the wars same as you, seen some terrible shit and lost two friends, you think I don't feel it? Maybe I just deal with that sort of shit better, maybe I just put it behind me and get on with life.'

'I don't know how you can do that,' said Adam. 'Put it

behind you and get on with life.'

'I just do,' said Roddy. 'What else is there to do? Jump in the fucking sea? What does that prove? Nothing, except that cunts like Joe and Grant have won, they've got to you so much you can't take it. I refuse to let those pricks win, and if you do by ending it all then you're just as big an arsehole as them.'

'Piss off, Hunter.'

'Fuck you, Strachan.'

Adam felt his blood heating up and surging wildly through his veins.

'This was all your fault anyway,' he said, voice rising.

'We've been over this fucking shit,' said Roddy. 'You're right to be angry, but not at me, dickhead.'

'If you hadn't been such a prick behind the wheel, none of this would've happened.'

'If, if, if,' said Roddy, exasperated. 'You can't live your life thinking about what-ifs. You just have to get on with it. Live your life, be a man of action for once.'

'A man of action?' Adam's vision went blurry, his muscles tensed, a burning sensation rose up in his throat.

'That's right.'

Adam grabbed Roddy and swung him round against the handrail. He punched Roddy's injured shoulder, making him cry out and crumple in pain, then pushed him back against the rail, bending him backwards over it. He had a hold of Roddy's coat and shook him with all his might, the wind gusting and whipping around them in a frenzy.

'What if I just throw you in right now!' He was screaming in Roddy's face, spit flying.

288

Roddy had an elated look on his face. 'That's the fucking stuff, let it all out.'

'Shut the fuck up.'

Roddy was grinning. 'If you push me over, I'll take you with me. Then we'll be fucking living, won't we? Until we drown, of course.'

'Maybe I really don't give a shit,' said Adam, keeping Roddy pinned. 'Maybe we both deserve to die.'

Roddy raised his eyebrows then spoke quietly. 'I don't think you mean that.'

Adam felt his resolve weaken and knew Roddy was right. He could feel his fury abating already, his hold of Roddy's coat loosening, the black fog of his mind clearing as he pictured the two of them tumbling over the side of the ferry and into the water, gripping each other until the force of the impact split them for ever.

He couldn't kill Roddy, just like he couldn't kill himself. He would have to keep living, with everything in his head, whether he liked it or not. A fucking life sentence.

He eased off on Roddy, let him back up, then finally let go of his coat and stepped away.

Roddy smiled, eyes wide. 'That was quite something, eh? Felt the blood pumping, didn't you? I know I fucking did.'

He rubbed his shoulder and grimaced, then pulled a bottle of pills out of his pocket. He shook out four and put them in his mouth. He got his hipflask out and took a glug to wash them down.

'Codeine,' he said. 'Got 'em by chatting up one of those nice nurses. Bollocks weak compared to the morphine, but they take the edge off. Fancy some?'

Adam looked at the bottle. Take the edge off. That sounded like something he could use.

'Why not.'

He popped four in his mouth and Roddy held out the hipflask.

'I got the barman downstairs to fill up with something special from under the bar,' he said. 'See if you can nail it.'

Adam shook his head but took the flask, swigging quickly to wash the pills down. He took a long sniff then another big sip, letting the malt roll around and over his tongue, his tasting skills kicking in instinctively. He lost himself in the process, letting the aromas curl over his tongue, the taste sensations coming at him thick and fast, a blast of salty sea breeze to match the wind buffeting them, huge flavours developing, sticky sweetness of toffee, a kick of mustard, oak smoke and worn leather. It was a thing of beauty, one of the finest malts he'd ever tasted, definitely one of the big guns.

'Ardbeg,' he said.

'Which one?'

'It's old. Maybe twenty-five years. From a vintage year like '74 or '77.'

Roddy smiled. 'Come on, then.'

'The '74 Provenance?'

Roddy shook his head. 'You are a fucking enigma, Strachan. I seriously don't know how you do it.'

Adam shrugged and took a big hit from the flask, this time drinking it straight down. He hoped it would warm his chest. He waited for the effect to kick in, but he still felt cold.

Roddy took the flask off him and put a hand on his shoulder.

'Come on, let's get in out of this fucking wind, I'm freezing my bollocks off out here.'

Roddy turned and went inside, holding the door open. Adam stared one last time out to sea then followed Roddy into the lounge.

Acknowledgements

Huge thanks to Trish, Allan, Ewan, Angus Cargill and everyone else at Faber.